Knights of the Boardroom

Book Two

Avery Gale

Knights of The Boardroom
Book Two
Copyright © October 2015 by Avery Gale
ISBN: 978-1-944472-21-4
Logo and all other art work © Copyright November 2015 by Avery Gale
All rights reserved.

Cover by Jess Buffett
Published by Avery Gale Books

Publisher's Note:
No part of this book may be reproduced, scanned, or distributed in any printed or electronic form without express written permission from the publisher. The scanning, uploading, and distribution of this book via the Internet or any other means without the permission of the publisher is illegal and punishable by law. Please do not participate in or encourage piracy of copyrighted materials in violation of the author's rights. Purchase only authorized editions.

Without limiting the rights under copyright reserved above, no part of this publication may be reproduced, resold (as a "used" e-book), stored or introduced into a retrieval system, or transmitted, in any form or by any means (electronic, mechanical, photocopying, recording or otherwise), without prior written permission of both the copyright owner and the above publisher of this book.

This book is a work of fiction. People, places, events, and situations are the product of the author's imagination. Any resemblance to actual persons, living or dead, or historical events, is purely coincidental.

WARNING: The unauthorized reproduction or distribution of this copyrighted work is illegal. Criminal copyright infringement, including infringement without monetary gain, is investigated by the FBI and is punishable by up to 5 years in federal prison and a fine of $250,000.

If you find any books being sold or shared illegally, please contact the author at avery.gale@ymail.com.

Dedication

This book is for every young woman who thinks her Knight misread the map and rode off in the wrong direction. There are times to listen with your head…but your heart will rarely lead you astray. Be patient. Don't settle.

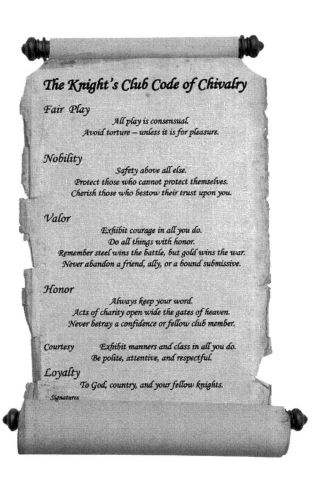

"Steel wins battles, but gold wins wars."

Prologue

CARLI WALKER WATCHED her sister's dress float around her like a soft cloud of color swirling in the breeze as she waltzed flawlessly across the polished marble floor of the ballroom with one of her new husbands. The dress reminded Carli of ribbons of fog and she considered for a moment whether or not those strips of translucent ivory fabric were the substance of the dress itself. Laughing to herself, she wondered when she'd dropped down the rabbit hole into Wonderland. Alice might have come across some strange things during her adventures beyond the looking glass, but having your younger sister transition from being a twenty-five year old virgin to marrying *two* of the richest men in the country ought to blow that damned Cheshire Cat right out of the water.

When Carli mentioned being worried Cressi's flushed cheeks and restlessness energy might indicate she wasn't feeling well, Tristan Harris smiled at her indulgently as he related in vivid detail what he considered a more likely explanation. Listening as one of the sexiest men she'd ever met explained the intricacies and effects of clit clips and nipple clamps was more than enough to make her soak her panties as her imagination took her right to the edge of her control. Tristan's voice was deep and resonate, the tone shifting so often she felt like half the story was being told by the pitch and timbre of his voice alone.

Feeling his warm hand wrap around her upper arm as he pulled her close and spoke against her ear made her entire body tremble. Each time she'd talked to him he'd called her *mon cher* and the easy way the French endearment rolled off his tongue made his familiarity seem like the most natural thing in the world. The man oozed sex on every level—he was incredibly handsome, but the sensuality that was infused in his every move was what drew her in. He was the very embodiment of the expression "sex on two legs" and the fluidity of his movements made her wonder how he'd be in bed. Tristan Harris was a titled, wildly wealthy British aristocrat, but he'd surprised her by being entirely humble anytime she'd talked to him— another huge plus in Carli's view.

The tingling sensation that moved over Carli's entire body intensified each time Tristan leaned over her shoulder or skimmed his fingers over her lower back. He'd moved to stand behind her, wrapping one arm just under her breasts. When he'd tightened the hold, it had lifted her barely covered breasts until she'd worried they were going to make a very public debut. Feeling the warm brush of air over the sensitive shell of her ear as he explained how Cressi's *Masters* were likely torturing her with pleasure made her own body yearn for that same intimacy. *Masters*—that was another point that amazed Carli. Knowing her younger sister was deeply immersed in the Dominant/submissive lifestyle with Lawton and Brodie was another piece of her sister's new life that mystified her.

How could her educated sister allow her husbands to control her every move? But when she'd asked her only sibling that question, Cressi had laughed at her. The new bride had simply waved Carli off before telling her when she was really ready to *listen* and *hear* what Cressi's life was like, then she'd be happy to share—but until then she'd admonished her older sister to keep her judgmental options to herself. Carli had reluctantly admitted Cressida certainly seemed to have found her voice since her life had changed so dramatically.

Feeling Tristan's rock hard pecs pressed against her back was going to fuel Carli's fantasies for months. Good Lord, she could feel the heat from his body despite the layers of clothing between them and it radiated clear to her soul. But the spell had been shattered when she'd mentioned the fact she needed to talk to her sister about a small security problem she'd had recently and Tristan had hustled her across the room like a petulant child. When she looked up to see Parker Daniels in front of her she tried to yank herself from Tristan's hold, and she could have sworn she'd heard the man growl at her. "He doesn't like me, why would you herd me over here like a naughty child?" She hadn't actually intended to speak loud enough for Tristan to hear, but she had obviously underestimated him. He'd stopped so quickly Carli had tripped over the hem of her gown and she would have been sprawled across the floor if Tristan hadn't caught her.

The man had the natural grace of a dancer and the lightning-quick reflexes that almost defied the laws of physics—*holy hell, how did he do that?* Tristan's movements had been little more than a blur, but he'd not only kept her from falling, he'd also spun her so they were now pressed tightly together chest to chest. This time when he spoke, she barely heard the words she was so distracted by their proximity. This close his eyes reminded her of the deepest blues of the Great Blue Hole off the coast of Belize—the color unlike any other she'd ever seen. The lush splendor of Belize drew her like a magnet, it was always one of her favorite locations to shoot despite the way the tropical humidity wreaked havoc with the natural curl in her hair. Every time her agency sent her to that small piece of heaven, her hairdressing team threatened mutiny. Until Tristan spoke, she hadn't even realized they were in a shadowed area of the ballroom, but it was his voice that pulled her back to the moment, "I don't know where you went, *mon cher,* but I love the way you fell into my eyes and appeared to be quite happy there. Now—tell me why you don't think Parker likes you—when I know for a fact that isn't true."

Carli was stunned—how could he have not noticed his friend's animosity toward her? Pulling back, she knew the only reason she was no longer plastered against him was because he'd allowed the distance. He kept her within arm's reach, but at least she was able to look into his eyes without having to strain her neck in the process. "Are you serious? The man only talks to me when he's mad about something I've done to screw up his security plans—plans that more often than not would make the Federal Bureau of Prisons proud. He barely tolerates me. Hell, I didn't even know he *could* smile until I saw him laying the charm on my sister. I swear he only deals with me to keep her happy. It isn't like he's going to give a rat's ass that Dale Roberts sent me roses this week."

The words had barely left her lips when she felt a heated chest press against her back. "There are so many lies in that dribble I'm not even sure where to start. Let's go, we need to talk." Parker and Tristan each took one of her hands to lead her from the room.

Digging in her heels, she protested, "Hey, I'm not going anywhere with you. Hell, you'll probably lock me in the nearest janitor's closet. So, thanks but no thanks. I think I'll stay right here were I'm in plain view of everyone." She hadn't really believed they'd lock her up—but the thought alone sent shards of ice racing through her blood—God in heaven she hated closed in dark spaces.

Her damned imagination was quickly getting the best of her and before she knew what was happening Parker and Tristan had adjusted their grip to her elbows and once again began making their way out of the enormous ballroom. "Best not make a scene, princess—I can assure you that your new brothers-in-law will not be thrilled if you upset their wife. They give a whole new meaning to overprotective."

Well, finally a point we seem to be in complete agreement on. The last thing she saw was her sister standing to the side giving her a thumbs up. *Good grief.*

Chapter One

WHEN WOULD SHE ever learn to keep her mouth shut? Giving an overzealous security chief ammunition to tighten the net he'd already dropped over her was definitely one of her dimmer moments. Carli Walker couldn't really claim she was surprised by Parker's reaction—but she was quite shocked at how quickly Tristan flipped a script on her. *Okay, maybe I need to stop hanging out with Phillip and his friends.* Picking up her art director's street slang probably wouldn't do much to preserve her reputation as one of the few supermodels who actually took an interest in the business side of her career. Phillip Gaines was not only one of her agency's best creative directors, he'd also become one of her dearest friends and closest confidants. They'd been a team since she'd first signed with the agency and each time she'd renegotiated her contract, keeping him close was one of the few points she refused to even discuss changing.

Phillip was brilliant, funny, and his preference for wild *boys* meant he'd been one of the few men in her life, under the age of sixty, who wasn't nice to her simply because he harbored an unrealistic expectation of getting her naked and underneath him. They'd become fast friends…always having one another's back, but even Phillip had threatened to notify the agency about the latest rash of craziness in her life if she didn't talk to them herself. Now she'd once again spouted off when she should have kept quiet...there just wasn't any way this was going to end well. *And if they think the roses are a problem, they were going to go apocalyptic about the masks.*

Feeling both men's grip tighten around her upper arms made Carli realize she had actually mutter those words out loud—*shit!* Damn it all to hell in a hand basket, speaking her thoughts aloud was a habit she'd had since she was a kid, and one that had gotten her grounded more times than she could count. Both men turned as one as if the move had been choreographed until they all three faced a set of large mahogany double doors—obviously they'd both known where they were headed. Too bad she hadn't gotten that particular memo, it would have given her more time to prepare her story.

Parker opened one of the heavy wooden doors and motioned her through, she hesitated because the room was shrouded in darkness. She'd never been comfortable in the dark and after her mother died, her young mind had associated death with eternal darkness, and if you added in a closed in space she usually launched straight into a full-blown meltdown. Over the years her "discomfort" had blossomed into an all-consuming fear that she tried very hard to hide from those around her.

Tristan must have sensed her trepidation because he opened the second door and stepped through, his movements activated the motion-controlled lights, and the room was instantly awash with a soft golden glow. Carli closed her eyes letting out an audible sigh of relief. When she opened her eyes Tristan was standing directly in front of her looking down, his expression considerate as he stroked the backs of his fingers across her cheek. "We'll be addressing your fear of the dark at some point, *mon cher*, but not today." She hadn't even realized she was leaning into his touch until he smiled and pressed a kiss to the center of her forehead. "You are going to be such a joy, love." She wasn't sure exactly what he meant, but before she could inquire he pulled her further into the room.

Carli took a moment to look around and drew in a sharp breath when she realized they were in the sitting room of a suite unlike any she'd ever seen. The hotel where the wedding reception was being held was the very definition of *gilded opulence*, but from her vantage point this suite took elegance to an entirely new level. The marble floors were shaded white with woven Persian rugs in subtle tones that highlighted the gold crown molding, giving the room a unique balance of color. The furnishings were an eclectic mix of heavy antique pieces and modern elements that spoke of both opulence and energy.

Earlier this evening when she'd first stepped out of enormous revolving door and into the five-star hotel's lobby, Carli had been swamped by the eerie sensation she'd been transported back in time—back to an era when moneyed ladies rode in covered horse drawn carriages and made their grand entrances into the ball by sweeping down the curved marble staircase. She'd never seen a staircase with such a large landing halfway to the top, it appeared to be something close to a small mezzanine and it made Carli want to explore every inch of the entire hotel.

When she'd first entered the large ballroom her eyes had been drawn to the intricate inlay pattern of the floor—she could have easily become mesmerized by the way the colors painted a maze unlike any other she'd ever seen. There were colors of marble and other stones she hadn't even known existed and it was humbling to think something so grand existed just a few blocks from the apartment she now had all to herself. Remembering that she now lived alone was a sobering thought. She'd been planning this transition for almost a year, and now—just when she would be traveling less, she was going to be alone. *Fuck me, I'm going to miss Cressi being sprawled over that ugly sofa she loves so much while some late night television hawker tries in vain to sell her a miracle cream guaranteed to erase the wrinkles she doesn't have.*

PARKER CONSIDERED HIMSELF a self-disciplined Dom, but staying focused on his need to address the dribble Carli had spouted off to Tristan in the ballroom was quickly losing out to his insane desire to strip her bare and fuck her seven ways to Sunday. Shaking his head, as if that was all it would take to erase the way her delicate hand had felt clasped in his own and negate the enticing, yet subtle fragrance she was wearing—*good God, she smells like a cool summer rain in the mountains*. He looked on as she took in her surroundings. Her expression was unguarded and appreciative as she studied the room with obvious appreciation, and her distraction gave him a moment to refocus his own wayward thoughts. He could almost hear her mentally tallying all the details of the spacious suite he'd reserved as soon as he'd known the venue for tonight's festivities. Actually *reserved* wasn't entirely accurate, because this particular suite was never available to anyone other than family members.

Templar's security team needed a space to set up, but they certainly hadn't needed the hotel owner's five-room suite. The two men he'd assigned to monitor the numerous cameras he'd added to the hotel's security system were tucked away in the smaller bedroom surrounded by a bank of monitors worthy of a space shuttle launch. The second bedroom had a separate entrance making it perfect for their needs—the men could be out the door in seconds if they were needed. His team of technicians had easily tapped into The Regency's system—something Parker intended to speak with the owner about before they moved out of the suite tomorrow morning.

J.T. Caine had owned The Regency for as long as Parker could remember, and even though the property was in pristine condition, their security system was definitely lacking. Right now J.T. and his third wife were vacationing in the Caribbean, but Parker wouldn't hesitate to call the man he'd known his entire life as Uncle J.T. and explain in unvarnished terms the problems he'd noted.

Reining in his own distracted thinking, Parker re-centered his attention on the beauty standing in front of him. The third time he spoke Carli's name, Parker deliberately used the tone no sub ever ignored and he was pleased when she quickly returned her focus to the two of them stammering, "Oh...umm, well...I'm sorry, what did you say?"

"Princess, I've been talking to you for a full minute—where the hell were you? And what was the last thing you were thinking about? The one that painted your entire demeanor with sadness?" They were going to clear this up first, then on to her comments in the ballroom.

"Oh, I was looking around the room—it's really lovely by the way. Then, you know...one thought led to another until I realized how much I'm going to miss living with Cressi. I know I wasn't there much but I'm finally to a point in my career where I can travel less...and it's really hard to come home to an empty apartment and know that's the way it's going to stay because no one will be joining you. I have no idea why she put up with me as a roommate for so long." Parker watched as she blinked back the tears filling her bright green eyes and fought the urge to pull her into his arms. If she belonged to him, he wouldn't want her to ever be home alone for any length of time—he and Tristan would be able to show her that particular advantage of ménage very easily. *I wonder how she'd feel about living on top of a kink club.* The fact he'd even considered the question startled him, and knowing he actually wanted to know the answer scared the hell out of him.

"Tell me about the roses." His voice was firm and commanding, and he was pleased to see she responded without any hesitation.

"Evidently they were delivered earlier this week, but I only got them very early this morning. They'd been left with the doorman in our building and he gave them to me when I raced through the lobby on my way upstairs to get ready for tonight's festivities. I saved the card but threw the flowers away because they were way past their prime—as I'm sure you can imagine. Roses just don't last as long as wildflowers." *Is she fucking kidding? The only reason she threw out flowers from her sister's stalker was because they were no longer fresh?*

"Mon cher, are you sure it was from Cressida's stalker? The last we knew, he was still out of the country." Parker could hear the concern in his friend's voice, they'd checked this afternoon and all the reports indicated Dale Roberts was still holed up in Indonesia. But the timing certainly made sense—when the object of a man's obsession married two of the country's most eligible bachelors, he might well want to spoil the celebration, but something about it didn't feel right to him.

"Well…not really. The little mask on the card made me wonder, but since I haven't had any of that particular trouble for a while…" Carli's voice faded to an uncomfortable silence at her unspoken reference to the threats she'd gotten a few months ago.

Goddammit to hell, why hadn't she called him immediately if she'd thought something was amiss? Because she thinks you don't like her, dumbass. People don't trust those who don't like them. Why would she call someone for help that she didn't trust? Thinking back on the challenges she'd had with NYPD, before her agency had brought him on board, it made perfect sense that Carli would shy away from anyone she thought wasn't fully vested in helping her.

Tristan gave him a look that was impossible to misinterpret—*yank your head out of your ass, I want her.* The warning wasn't necessary, Parker knew Tristan Harris well enough to see the desire in his eyes—and even though he considered their plan to *share* a woman *someday* a given, it might well be a point he and Tristan needed to discuss in depth once again. And as unpleasant as it was to admit, Parker wanted her too—no matter how badly he wished things were different. Taking a deep breath hoping the extra oxygen would smooth out the frustration he feared would be too easy to hear in his tone, Parker simply said, "Tell us about the mask."

Before she had a chance to respond, his phone vibrated in the breast pocket of his suit jacket. Pulling it out, he had an immediate feeling of dread—the only reason one of his men would be calling, rather than using the comm device they were all wearing, was if something significant had happened. Curt was his second in command and knew where he was, so he'd only be calling if he had information he didn't think his boss would want to share with the entire team.

Holding up one finger, gesturing her to hold tight a minute, Parker listened as Curt explained they'd had two unexpected floral deliveries. "It seemed odd to me because Dr. Hill had already given us a list of all the venders and this courier service wasn't on the list. So when the first arrangement arrived we set it aside and didn't take it into the ballroom. Then when the second one showed up a few minutes ago, I became even more suspicious and disassembled both of them. What I found was interesting to say the least—remote controlled cameras without storage capabilities so I know they were broadcasting, even though I haven't had time to do much with them yet. And here's another thing—both cards have a strange drawing on them."

Parker was wondering if their Intel had been wrong—perhaps Dale Roberts was indeed back stateside, until Curt's mention of small drawings on both cards caught his attention. "Drawings? What sort of drawings?"

"Masks. They weren't exactly the same, but they were the same style and both definitely masks—the sort you associate with theatre, you know those masks your grandmother had hanging in her music room."

What the hell? My granny has posters of musicians—from Frank Sinatra to Alice Cooper hanging in her music room.

"Actually I think I know what you are talking about, even though my grandmother has somewhat eclectic musical tastes, so none of that sort of thing for her." He couldn't hold back his mental laugh as he thought about his paternal grandmother—Deedra Daniels was five foot nothing and Parker was absolutely certain he'd never met anyone more full of joyful nonsense—although Lilly West regularly gave Granny Daniels a run for her money—it was easy to see why the two women had been life-long friends. As far as Parker had ever been able to see, his granny lived her life by her own rules, steadfastly refusing to *grow-up* despite her son's numerous hints that she needed to. In Parker's opinion, it was his dad's insistence that she also needed to *slow down* that ensured her militant resistance.

The last time he'd listened as his dad had tried to persuade Granny that Houston's newest retirement village would be perfect for her, he'd laughed out loud at the look of horror on her face. "Sonny, I am *not* moving in with a bunch of old people, they are God-awful boring, you know." She'd turned to Parker and winked, "Don't ever grow up, baby boy—it's a trap." Parker might have laughed out loud at the time, but he hadn't doubted for a hot minute she was right.

Ending the call, Parker turned to Carli and apologized, "Sorry about the interruption, now—tell me about the masks."

Carli wrapped her arms around herself making Parker wondered if she was cold or if she was shielding herself from some unpleasant memory—hell, maybe she was hiding from his appreciative gaze. "I don't really know what to tell you except the damned things started showing up everywhere. It was so weird—I'd see them on Post-it notes in the hallways at shoots, on the mirrors in dressing rooms, in the windows of stores where I shopped, the elevator in my apartment building…always in places I couldn't imagine any one person being responsible for their placement because the locations were so diverse."

Neither Parker nor Tristan replied, as experienced Doms they understood the value of being patient. Parker noticed the muscle in Tristan's jaw twitching and wanted to laugh—the man had a real issue with women cursing, something he didn't doubt he'd get to watch play out in vivid color between the two people standing in front of him.

They watched as she rubbed the silky fabric of her dress slowly between her fingers looking for all the world like she was a thousand miles away—lost in her own thoughts. While she'd been speaking Carli had wandered to the white marble fireplace mantle, tracing her French-tipped nails along the edge in a way that made him wonder what those slender fingers would feel like wrapped around his cock. *Goddammit, Daniels, get your head out of your ass.* He was about to concede defeat when she suddenly looked up, fear easy to see in her eyes, "The only possible answer is that it's someone in my inner circle—and that scares the hell out of me."

Parker closed the distance between them until he was less than an arm's length in front of her before using his fingers to lift her chin forcing her to look directly into his eyes, "Carli, do you trust me to keep you safe?" The question was direct enough he hoped she would answer, because he certainly wasn't going to ask her if she felt safe with him, the connotations of that particular question were entirely different. Had he ever wanted something so much even though he knew it was going to lead to nothing but trouble?

For the past year his parents, grandparents, and friends had *all* been nagging him about his *love 'em and leave 'em* lifestyle. Hell, even Tristan had made it clear—more than once—it was time for them to find a woman and settle down…spouting off crap about his biological clock of all the asinine things. Parker's comment about his best friend turning into a pussy had ended up with them sparring in the club's gym, and despite the additional two inches in height and thirty pounds—Tristan had handed him his ass in short order. *Fucking James Bond wannabe. The man needs a woman in his life, maybe he'll stop all the damned hand-to-hand combat training.*

"Yes." Her eyes hadn't left his, there was conviction in her voice when she'd answered, but there was also a hesitance he couldn't identify, and for some reason that bothered him. When he simply raised a brow at her in question she deflated, shoulders drooping—hell, her entire posture changed. "Of course I know you can keep me safe, but I shouldn't need you to. I shouldn't be afraid to go home—it's not like I'm looking forward to living alone, but I hate being afraid of what I'll find anytime I step through the door."

Find? What the hell?

Chapter Two

TRISTAN MOVED TO stand behind Carli so quickly she squeaked in surprise. Wrapping her in his embrace, he pressed his nose into her hair letting the sweet scent of her shampoo and warm woman soak to the very depths of his soul. He wasn't sure who he was trying to comfort, himself or Carli, but for those few seconds, it didn't matter because she felt so perfect in his arms. *This should be your refuge, mon amore.* Tristan didn't know Carli well, but the one thing he knew to the depths of his soul was that he'd be able to spend a lifetime peeling back the layers of Carli Walker and never feel like he'd uncovered every one of her secrets. She'd stiffened when he'd first enfolded her into his arms but she'd soon relaxed, and knowing she'd accepted his comfort filled a place inside him he'd known for a long time was far too empty.

Leaning down, he spoke close to her ear, "The party is going to start winding down soon, but neither of us are finished talking to you about this...not by a long shot. I suggest we return to the party before the bride and grooms say their goodbyes—something I'm sure you don't want to miss. After that, we can go to my place to continue this discussion, including the fact from this point forward you'll be held accountable for cursing—so don't. You've already been to my home, so it will be comfortable for you." He'd deliberately stated it *would be* comfortable rather than should be in an effort to set the tone for her return. Tristan's favorite memory of his bedroom was watching Carli Walker sleeping in his bed the night she'd shown up at the club looking for her sister.

From the little bit he'd heard of Parker's earlier phone conversation, he was betting there had already been some sort of security breach so there wasn't a snowball's chance in hell they'd let her return home alone. His American mother would be proud of him for finally fully understanding the meaning of that expression. The first time he remembered hearing her use it, Tristan had wondered if his mom's free spirit hadn't finally flown the coop taking her good sense with it. But he'd learned over time how fond Americans were of overstating the obvious to make a point, so he'd finally understood what she'd been trying to say.

"We need to get some answers now." Parker's voice had broken the spell of the moment and Tristan wanted to roll his eyes at his petulant tone. He wouldn't let his friend turn this into a power struggle—at least not until they'd made Carli theirs, then the two of them could tussle all they wanted to because they would all know how it would end. For now, there needed to be compromises—a lot of compromises. Tristan leveled a look at this friend that should have singed his brows, before stepping to the side to pull the small toy bag he'd brought out from behind the sofa. When Parker realized what Tristan had in his hand, he furrowed his brow looking both surprised and confused at the same time.

Palming a pair of steel Ben Wa Balls, Tristan stepped back behind Carli. Looking down, he couldn't help but smile at the dress she was wearing—*perfect*. "Since I know

Carli would like to get back to her sister's reception before she misses their exit *and* I know Parker wants to continue this conversation, I want to play a game."

"What's your plan?" Parker's words had been directed to Tristan, but his eyes hadn't left Carli.

Pressing a kiss to the sensitive spot below Carli's ear, Tristan answered, "I say we let her earn her time back in the ballroom. If she agrees to wear what I have in my hand, we escort her back to the party until her sister leaves—or until she decides she is ready to go back to my place where we can continue." He'd been deliberately vague about what they'd continue, because he was confident the little balls tucked into his palm would completely scatter her focus. And with her attention *elsewhere*, Parker would be able to get quick, honest answers to his questions. As the manager of The Knight's Club, Tristan had seen Doms use similar methods many times when getting to the root of a problem quickly was imperative...desperate desire was a great truth serum.

"What do you say, princess? You up to Master Tristan's challenge?" Parker's voice was so close to taunting, Tristan wondered if Carli would simply walk away. She could—they had no real reason to detain her, although he was sure her two new brothers-in-law would give it a good go if it came to down to that. But Tristan also felt her spine straighten—*oh yeah, she was going to meet his challenge*. This would be a battle she was very much going to enjoy losing, he planned to make sure of it.

Tristan wanted to laugh out loud when he saw her pretty little chin tilt up a split second before she said, "Bring it, Parker. I think you two are bluffing—I'm not like Cressi, I'm not going to be overwhelmed by your more advanced sexual experience."

Words every Dom loves to hear, baby. Challenge accepted.

Sliding his arm around her waist, Tristan pulled Carli back until she was pressed so tightly against him it would be impossible for her to miss the effect she was having on him. Hearing her breath catch was music to his ears. Loosening his hold to turn her so he could see her face, he asked, "Do you have a safe word, *mon cher*?"

"I...why would I need one? Are you planning to hurt me?" Tristan heard a mixture of fear and hope in her voice—oh yeah, Carli was more like her sister than she believed herself to be.

"Safe words are about more than pain, baby. We'll use the club's stop light system. Green means you are good to go. If you are feeling anxious or are beginning to feel uncomfortable and want to take a break, use yellow. We'll stop and let you ask questions, keep in mind we may or may not answer, but I can assure you we will listen to your concerns even if we don't alter our plan. If you find yourself so overwhelmed, either physically or emotionally that you cannot continue, simply say *red* and everything stops."

Tristan fought his smile as Carli stood blinking at him with the most adorable look of confusion he'd ever seen. When she didn't respond, Parker stepped closer and spoke softly to her, "Princess? You need to let us know you understand what Master Tristan just explained. This is one of the most fundamental elements of our lifestyle, nothing happens without your consent—open and honest communication is the only way we can be sure you are making informed decisions."

Some of the fog seemed to clear from Carli's eyes as she listened to Parker, and she finally whispered, "Yes, I understand. I've read a lot about Dominance and submission, because…well, because of Cressi."

Tristan tightened his arm around her once again…just enough to gain her attention, "Don't lie to us, Carli. We'll always know." He turned her so slowly in his arms he knew she'd have felt the steel length of his erection pressing against her hip and ass cheeks—another reminder of how much he was looking forward to their time together.

Her breathing sped up at his warning and Tristan grinned at Parker over her head. Evidently she was one of those wonderful women who found it almost impossible to lie effectively—lucky them. He'd be willing to bet she'd been reading about the lifestyle long before her sister's relationship with Lawton and Brodie. Now he was curious how far she'd gone in her exploration, just thinking about another Dom having trained her made him see red.

Pressing a lingering kiss against the sweet spot below her ear, Tristan noted that her pulse was racing and he wondered if he could talk her over the edge of orgasm. Thinking about all the places he could practice that particular skill made his cock bob in encouragement. "So are you ready for this challenge, *mon cher*? While you're wearing my *gift*, I'd like nothing more than to take you back into the party and dance with you. Holding you in my arms as we move together to the music sounds like a lovely way to spend time before we can get you alone." He felt her shudder against him and the low moan he knew had started deep in her chest made him wonder how that sound would feel vibrating around his cock as he slid between her full lips.

"Yes, I need to get back to the reception before Cressi starts worrying." Tristan wanted to tell her that he'd seen her sister's thumbs up sign as they'd left so it was doubtful the little imp was worrying about Carli's safety, but he kept the remark to himself. He'd make sure she had a chance to speak with her sister briefly before Law and Brodie whisked her away, Cressi might not notice the distraction the two weighted steel balls would cause Carli, but her men certainly would. Even though Carli Walker was one of the most photographed women in the world, she wasn't ready for the kind of attention a scream-the-walls-down public orgasm would attract, so he planned to carefully monitor her once they returned to the party. Oh, he fully intended for her to come apart in his arms while they were dancing—after all, didn't people refer to dancing as sex set to music?

When he started to gather the fabric of her dress raising the hem so he could slip his hand underneath, he appreciated the fact she'd chosen a full skirt rather than a skin-tight gown. The layers of chiffon all appeared to have slightly different floral prints giving the garment a visual depth that reminded him of the English gardens he'd grown up enjoying. Skimming his palm up the outside of her toned thigh, Tristan pressed a kiss against her temple, "Your skin is so soft, baby. I can't wait to trace that same path with my lips—I'll taste every inch of you as soon as you'll let me. There won't be a spot I won't know. Open for me."

Carli's head had fallen to the side, an instinctual move of submission as old as time itself. She'd bared the side of her throat to him and he intended to reward the small sign she'd given herself over to him. Biting down gently at the place where her neck and shoulder met, Tristan was pleased to feel goose flesh race over the surface of her skin. Carli's responses were perfect—Tristan hoped Parker realized how wonderfully she responded to his touch, one glance in his friend's direction confirmed he had indeed noticed. Parker's attention was centered on Carli, the desire easy to see in his eyes. She slid her feet apart, not as much as he'd demand if she belonged to him, but he knew once he started sliding his fingers through the slick petals of her pussy her legs would part further of their own volition.

"You know, Parker, this beautiful woman isn't wearing any panties. I do believe she was made for us."

"Lines…I didn't want any lines."

"Princess, that is a very full skirt, I can't imagine lines being a huge issue." Parker's half grin was more taunt than amusement, and it didn't seem lost on the lovely woman in his arms. When he felt her stiffen, he slid the tips of two fingers just inside her channel. It was definitely time to distract her before she and Parker decided to argue rather than play.

"God save me, you are so wet, *mon cher*. And smooth as drenched silk—I love that you are waxed, baby." Tristan slid his entire palm over her smooth sex wondering how sweet she was going to taste. He'd always dreamed of having the kind of soul-deep connection with a woman that he saw between his parents and when he'd asked his dad about it one night, his typically easy-going father had become uncharacteristically solemn. He'd taken so long to answer, Tristan had begun to think he wasn't going to.

William Harris had always lived an incredibly privileged life, so his words that night had been particularly poignant. "I'd never known what peace felt like until I held your mother in my arms. It was as if everything around me aligned perfectly for the first time—all the pieces that had been scattered over the playing board that was my life, fell into place and I could see my future so clearly it was as if she'd painted it on canvas."

Tristan hadn't responded, not because he didn't believe

his father's proclamation, but because he was speechless—he hadn't expected such heartfelt candor. William Harris might not have always been as carefree and flamboyant as his beautiful American wife, but she had a way of pulling people into her enthusiasm. Tristan wanted the same sort of all-encompassing love that he'd seen demonstrated each and every day while growing up. And even though Parker might not think he was ready for love, the spark between his best friend and the woman in his arms was going to be the fuel that fed that flame.

TRISTAN'S WARM BREATH brushing over the shell of her ear made her knees so weak she wasn't sure how much longer they would hold her upright. Somewhere in the back of her lust-fogged mind, Carli realized Tristan was holding her tightly against his chest. She was so lost in the sensations racing through her body, she couldn't seem to pull the thoughts all together, and for a woman who was well accustomed to having hot men close to her during photo shoots, that was saying a lot.

She'd just started to think she might come from his words alone...and then his fingers slid between her legs and her orgasm loomed so close it became a question of *when* rather than *if*. She'd been floating happily in a sea of pleasure as the waves started building quickly like a musical piece working toward a monumental crescendo that she hadn't been focused on his words until somewhere in the back of her mind it registered he'd said something about her being waxed. Shaking her head, she moaned softly, "No. Waxing hurts." She knew she'd barely whispered the words, but Tristan had obviously heard them because his fingers stopped their sensual caress for just a second before continuing.

"*Mon amour*, I know smooth skin as well as any Master, and yours is perfect. There are very few ways to make your pussy this wonderfully smooth. Tell me." God in heaven his voice had to be that of an angel sent to earth just to torture women.

Carli found herself fighting back to the surface of awareness in her attempt to answer. In truth she was impressed as hell she'd found enough functioning brain cells to form the two words she needed, "Laser treatments," was all she managed to say before being blindsided by an orgasm so powerful she actually saw small bursts of light behind her eyelids. Her mind was muddled, but she'd felt him slip something inside her before her body had stopped convulsing around his fingers.

"You soaked my hand with your cream and I can hardly wait to taste you, baby. Just feeling that creamy rush of warmth flow over my hand was enough to make me rethink our plan to return to the party. I'd much rather bend you over the enormous bed in the master suite and fuck you until neither one of us is capable of walking back down the hall." His voice had gone so deep she could almost feel the dark intensity she was certain surrounded him at The Knight's Club.

Carli had heard enough of her sister's stories about Lawton's and Brodie's sexual inclinations, and from everything she'd heard the two men standing on either side of her were far more dedicated to the lifestyle than her sister's husbands. Cressi insisted her men had mellowed a lot because she was still so new to BDSM practices, but from Carli's point of view, it appeared the two men who had once been her younger sister's bosses were so over the moon that there wasn't anything they wouldn't do for their lovely bride.

"Who did your laser treatments?" Carli was startled back to the moment by Tristan's question. *Did I tell him I was doing laser treatments?* She'd actually been finished before she'd decided recently to go for a full Brazilian.

"Carli? I believe Master Tristan asked you a question. It's in your best interest to answer questions immediately and with complete honesty—and since you've already stated you won't be overwhelmed by us, I don't see it being an issue, do you?" Damn, he had a way of getting under her skin in no time at all. Honestly, she wondered if it wasn't some sort of challenge to him. *Drown him, this really isn't any of their business, but if I tell them that I'm never going to get back to the party.*

"I've just started them again a few months ago and I'm finished with the…umm, well, the additional work I wanted done. Well, I'll go back for a follow up or two for touchups, but that's it. Leo at Cynthia's is my laser esthetician." She was surprised when Parker simply nodded. She'd been expecting a battle and was pleasantly surprised to have evidently dodged that particular bullet.

"Now, let's get back to the party—I believe I'm in the mood to dance." The teasing tone of Tristan's words didn't make any sense to her until she took the first few steps toward what she hoped was a restroom. Holy fucking hell, whatever he'd slid inside her was lighting her up from the inside and after just a few steps, she found herself grasping the edge of a nearby table to keep from weaving on her feet. She had no idea how he'd managed it, but Tristan's arm banded around her waist so quickly she wondered for just a moment if he hadn't actually been right behind her anticipating her reaction. "Where exactly where you headed, *mon cher?*"

"I'd be willing to bet she thought she was going to the restroom to wipe away all that sweet honey coating those smooth pussy lips—you didn't think we'd let you wipe away the evidence of how much you enjoyed that little scene, did you, princess?" *Oh indeed I did.* Carli didn't know how Parker had figured out her plan, but it was plain to see he was going to be difficult to fool—hell, they were both forces of nature. She was definitely going to have to step up her game to maintain any sort of control. *Well, game on, boys.*

Chapter Three

CRESSIDA WAS GETTING worried about her sister. When she'd first seen them leaving, she had assumed the men were finally acting on their obvious interest in Carli, but then she'd noted their stern expressions. She'd seen that look on her own men's faces on several occasions and knew well what it meant, and Carli had been gone far too long for Parker and Tristan to have been simply asking her questions. Cressi knew her sister well enough to be certain she wouldn't sleep with the two of them during the party, not that Carli Walker was a nun by any means, but she'd always been incredibly discrete about her sex life. Carli had always insisted she saw no reason to give the public any additional reasons to judge her.

Trying to casually slip out of the room had proven difficult since neither of her husbands had missed Carli's exit with Parker and Tristan, they'd barely let her out of their sight since. The first time she'd tried to make an escape, Brodie had wrapped his arm around her turning her into his chest so quickly she'd stumbled against him. "Where do you think you are going, pet?" His words had wafted over the back of her neck as he leaned down and pressed a kiss against her sweat-dampened skin. Between her new fathers-in-law and her husbands, she'd barely been off the dance floor all evening and she was edging toward exhaustion.

"To check on my sister and freshen up a bit. I could also use something to drink." Her words didn't have the solid sound of commitment she'd intended, but damn the man could distract her just by being close.

She felt his hum of satisfaction vibrating through his chest as he pressed himself tightly against her and drew his tongue across her damp skin. "No need to freshen up, pet, I happen to like you hot and sweaty, sweet wife of mine. It means Lawton and I are doing our job, even if our fathers can't seem to keep their hands off you." Good God the man oozed sensuality on a level that probably should come with a warning label. Cressi didn't think there was a straight woman on the planet immune to Brodie's charm. She'd seen him use it on women of all ages—and was well accustomed to seeing the dazed look in their eyes after they'd been hit with the full force of what she affectionately referred to as "The Brodie Effect".

"While I love being hot and sweaty with you, dear husband mine—I doubt it's attractive to our guests."

"Hmm, that is probably a statement I could refute, but I'll concede the point since arguing with you isn't what I have in mind for later." She chuckled at his words because God knew they'd debated far less significant minutia before—the fact he was a brilliant attorney and she a paralegal set them up as verbal adversaries on a regular basis.

"Good to know we're on the same page about *later*, but for now—if you'll excuse me." She tried to step back out of his hold, but he didn't release her.

"Come. I'll show you to a more private powder room upstairs." Drat, how was she supposed to snoop around if he went along? Ordinarily she found their care and attention comforting, but there were times—*like now*—when it was downright inconvenient.

Thirty minutes later, after several more dances, Cressida was making another attempt to escape the ballroom when she felt a warm hand wrap around her wrist and knew without even looking it was Lawton. "Where are you off to, baby?"

Sighing to herself, there wasn't any way to avoid the truth since she knew the two of them would have already compared notes, so the *freshen up* excuse wasn't going to work again. "I'm going to look for Carli. She's been gone an awfully long time." Best to keep it simple, less to defend later.

With practiced ease he spun her effortlessly into his embrace, his arms wrapping around her as she pressed her cheek against his chest...and waited for the questions she was sure were coming, and as if on cue, she heard him sigh as he leaned back, "Look at me, Cressida." He so rarely used her name anymore that it surprised her into complying immediately, even though they weren't in a twenty-four seven D/s relationship, her inner submissive always responded to that tone of voice. When her eyes finally met his, they reflected a softer temperament than she'd expected, "Do you trust us, baby? Do you trust that your happiness is the most important thing to your husbands and Masters?"

"Yes." Cressi didn't have to think about her answer, because she believed with all her heart that the two of them would protect her with everything they had. Although her ideas and theirs about what would make her happy were not always perfectly in sync.

"Then why would you think we would let anything happen to your sister? She is important to you—therefore she is important to us. And don't think for a minute she isn't safe with Parker and Tristan—they'd never hurt her, but I think you already know that."

"Maybe not physically...or intentionally, but that doesn't mean it might not happen."

"Sweetheart, life is full of risks—anyone who steers clear of all the chances life throws their way never gets to experience the exhilaration a leap of faith can bring. You can't truly appreciate the best life has to offer unless you have experienced—or at least seen some of the worst—that's what gives people perspective." Cressi felt herself deflate like a popped balloon. How was she supposed to argue with him when doing so was going to be tantamount to saying she didn't trust them? She finally nodded her head even though there was still a large part of her that worried about her sister.

Carli may have traveled the world, but she was also very insulated by a small group of assistants who traveled with her. They made her reservations, secured her travel documents, set up the itinerary, ordered her meals, and shopped for her so she wasn't mobbed by the locals—in short, they took care of everything. Carli had often likened herself to a mannequin, insisting she had about as much power as one as well. Cressida knew Carli often considered herself a virtual prisoner locked in beautiful cells disguised as opulent hotel suites, and for the past six months Carli had seemed particularly frustrated with the way she was kept "under a net" as she'd described it.

Lawton leaned down and pressed a kiss against her lips and Cressi felt herself slide a little further under his spell. But before he completely derailed her, she asked, "Could you walk me upstairs to the powder room, please? I'm getting tired and I really should have skipped those last sips of champagne. What on earth was that anyway? It tasted like apple cider." Lawton's expression blanked so quickly she started to ask him why, wondering if they hadn't switched out her drinks to control her alcohol intake. But her sweet husband distracted her with a toe-curling kiss that left her panting before he led her up the lobby's beautiful marble staircase. She'd been up the stairs earlier with Brodie, but she hadn't taken time to appreciate the grandeur and old world elegance of the space. There was a small sitting area halfway up the stairs and just as they arrived there, someone at the bottom of the stairs called Lawton's name.

"Stay here, baby, I'll be right back." He quickly descended the stairs but stayed where she could see him. She recognized the man he was speaking with as one of Templar Enterprises Group's security team and from the look on their faces, neither man was pleased with whatever had happened. Turning to look at the enormous painting of a woman riding in an ornate horse drawn carriage, Cressi came face to face with someone in a mask that looked like something you'd find in a vintage trunk of a college drama department.

A disembodied voice spoke from behind the mask, "This is for your sister," just before Cressi was shoved so hard she lost her balance and felt herself teetering on the top step for several seconds. Time seemed to slow to a crawl as Cressida pin wheeled her arms, frantically trying to regain control of her upper body, but her center of gravity was pitched too far backward. She heard Lawton shouting her name from the bottom of the stairs, but Cressi knew there wasn't any way he could make it to her in time. As she fell backward, Cressida felt the scream vibrate through her chest as she watched her attacker sprint up the stairs away from her. When her head hit the marble, Cressi heard a loud crack just as a blinding pain sent her into a dark abyss of silent relief.

LAWTON LISTENED AS Curt explained they'd had two unscheduled floral deliveries for Carli, what they'd found inside, and the updated security protocol. He watched as a small-framed figure wearing a dark hoodie approach his wife, but before he could even step around Curt, everything was already in motion. He'd only cleared the first few steps when he heard Cressida's earsplitting scream seconds before the crack of her skull colliding with the marble step echoed down the stairs. Watching as she went completely limp, tumbling down several more steps like a rag doll was something he was certain would haunt him for the rest of his life. Lawton could hear people all around him shouting instructions to call 911 and giving chase to the man or woman who'd attacked Cressida, but his focus was on the crumpled form laying at his feet. Just as he reached for her, Curt stopped him, "We shouldn't move her any more than necessary. I'm worried we'll further injure her."

Crouching down beside her, Lawton pressed his fingers against the side of her neck and was relieved to feel her pulse—it wasn't as strong as it should have been, but it was there and he was trying to focus on that. They were immediately surrounded by people, but the only voice he heard was Brodie's, "What the fuck happened?"

"Get my mother." To his credit, Brodie didn't hesitate, he turned on his heel and was gone before Lawton could blink. Lawton's mom might be a cardiologist, but she'd know all the emergency procedures necessary to triage and would also be able to make the calls necessary to get the best people in place at the hospital. Glancing up seconds later, Lawton wasn't surprised to see his mom sprinting up the stairs barefoot—she'd no doubt ditched her heels in the interest of speed.

Dr. Lana Hill was a hurricane when she was in doctor mode and she was already shouting orders into her phone as she knelt at Cressida's side. "Bernie, I don't give two shits if you aren't on call—this is my daughter-in-law and I want *you*." She paused briefly as she brushed her fingers gently over Cressida's cheek, and then nodded as if the man on the other end of the call could actually see her, "Yes, EMS is on the way and I'm going to assess now. I'll update you on the way in. And, Bernie...thanks, this young woman is important to all of us."

Law didn't wait to be asked, he just launched right into a rundown of what had happened. His mom didn't ask many questions because he'd given her everything he knew she would need. The paramedics were there quickly and Lawton found himself pushed back away from Cressida's side—and he'd never felt so helpless in his entire life. Turning to Brodie, he asked, "Did anyone catch up with the asshole who pushed her?"

"No. Whoever it was obviously had a well thought out plan for escape because he disappeared without a trace. Parker and his team are reviewing the security tapes now, and Tristan has been tasked with trying to contain Carli." The last Lawton had seen, the pair had been dancing in the shadows of the ballroom. Cressida hadn't seen them reenter the party and Lawton had recognized his friends' body language. Both men were in full Dom mode, so he hadn't wanted to spoil their fun.

Now, in hindsight, he wished like hell he'd ratted the

bastards out, then perhaps he and Brodie wouldn't be looking on as their wife was strapped to a damned backboard. Brodie spoke from his side, "Don't. Don't blame yourself for this. When someone wants to hurt another person, they'll go to incredible lengths to make it happen. I know you…and I'm sure you never let her out of your sight. We can't lock her away and protect her from every possible harm—no matter how much we may want to."

Lawton let out the breath he hadn't even realized he was holding, "Did you call for the car? There won't be room in the ambulance for us and I want to be ready to roll as soon as they do. They'll take her to New York-Presbyterian, Mom was already calling in people before she got up the stairs." Brodie's quick nod assured him their car was already waiting. They followed the first responders down the stairs and watched as they loaded Cressida in the back of the waiting ambulance.

His mom pressed a quick kiss to his cheek, muttered a few assurances about taking care of the love and light of his life as she climbed into the back—and then they were gone. Brodie nudged him with his shoulder toward their waiting car and within seconds they were right behind the ambulance as it made its way toward the hospital. For the first time in too many years, Lawton prayed. It wasn't that he didn't believe in God—he'd been raised in the church and had a deep respect for the good that came out of the charities they sponsored. But as he'd grown up, he'd discovered too many people used their faith as a weapon and he hadn't been able to reconcile that with his personal beliefs, so he'd slowly drifted away. And it wasn't until this moment that he'd realized the only person he'd hurt with that distance was himself. He'd denied himself the strength he'd felt in that connection—it wasn't about a church or a doctrine, it was about the stability and inner peace that came from believing in something bigger than yourself.

Lawton didn't care if it made him seem desperate—he was going to seek help any place he might be able to find it. The woman lying unconscious in the ambulance in front of them was more important than any ideological argument or his own pride...she held his heart in the palm of her hand, there wasn't anything he wouldn't do for her and he knew Brodie felt the same way.

CARLI MANAGED TO stay on her feet dancing in the shadowed areas of the ballroom and all things considered, that was enough of an accomplishment that she was actually proud of herself. She hadn't gotten a chance to dance with Parker, he'd been called away moments before she and Tristan had finished their first dance. Tristan hadn't missed a beat, he'd simply spun her around seamlessly moving into the next dance. She'd stumbled and almost fallen, but it hadn't been due to the change of music—no, whatever he'd put inside of her shifted each time she moved and the vibrations deep in her core were stealing every bit of her concentration. Hell, she'd barely been able to walk back down the hall to the party.

She'd wanted to find Cressi right away, but Tristan had insisted they dance first and it hadn't taken her long to figure out why. In fact she was grateful he'd persisted because she wasn't sure she would have been able to conceal the fact she was more than a little unfocused. "Tell me what you're thinking, *mon cher.*"

Tristan's words startled her—another testament to the fact she wasn't as self-aware as she needed to be. "I was just thinking it might have been hard to hide my distraction from my sister. She would have asked a lot of intrusive questions without giving the fact we're in a relatively public venue a second thought. Typical little sister behavior, but to be honest, she has gotten a lot bolder since her relationship with Lawton and Brodie changed."

"How so?" Even in the dim light, Carli could see his blue eyes dancing with the mischievous light of someone who already knew the answer to the question he was asking.

Carli had to take several deep breaths to pull herself back from the edge when Tristan dipped her during the few seconds between one song and the next. As the vibrations in her core ebbed slightly she continued, "I'm not really sure how to explain it—but she is different, more confident now than she was before." She really was trying to concentrate on their conversation, but her body was totally focused on something else entirely, and her brain was quickly losing the battle for supremacy.

Tristan was a wonderful dancer and she enjoyed the ease with which he led her around the small area where he seemed content to stay. "You look flushed, are you feeling all right?" The wicked grin on his face let her know he knew exactly what she was feeling. *Rat bastard.* His hand came down across her ass in a solid swat that sent scorching heat skittering over her skin, but the effect on the inside was devastating. "You're going to regret slandering my mother when you meet her—she's a delightful woman, even if she can be a bit of a wildcard at times." *Holy shit, I said that out loud?* When he leaned down and kissed the side of her neck she missed a step in the dance causing him to tighten his hold on her and caution, "Careful, sweetness. Tell me how your body is reacting to the balls. Are they vibrating together and setting your core on fire, because I can smell your arousal and *that* is certainly having a profound effect on me."

Ben Wa Balls—she'd read about them, but had never had the courage to buy them for herself. Obviously everything she'd read had been true because she was all too aware of the fact her body was seconds from tipping over the edge and when it did, there wasn't going to be anything she could do to stop the orgasm that had been building since she'd taken those first steps with the balls in place. Before she realized what was happening, he'd backed up to a wall deep in the shadows. Her back was to the room—which surprised her, until she realized his hand was gliding up her thigh. His palm left a trail of scorching heat against her naked legs as he slid his fingers smoothly to the juncture of her thighs. He didn't hesitate to slide the tips of his fingers leisurely through her wet folds.

"Oh, *mon cher*, you are so wet and so sweetly wanton. I cannot tell you how perfect you are for us." She started to argue, but when she opened her mouth, the only thing that came out was a moan. "Oh, music to my ears, *mon amour*, but right now I'm not of a mind to share that sweet sound with all the other guests who are so close." *Guests? Close? Damn.* She wasn't sure she would be able to keep quiet if he made her come. *If?*

"Please." Carli wasn't even sure what she was asking for, she'd never had an orgasm that she hadn't been personally responsible for until a half hour ago. And if that was any indication, there wasn't much chance she was going to be quiet this time either. "I don't want to—to make a scene, but oh…please."

His eyes flashed with desire so strong she saw it shine through the dim light a split second before he sealed his lips over hers and pushed his fingers in just deep enough to press against the small magical spot that lit her up like the Fourth of July. His tongue mimicked the movement of his fingers, plunging in before retreating and then pushing relentlessly forward once again. Over and over he repeated the unpredictable pace that kept her right on the precipice. Her entire body was vibrating with desperation, something he must have seen in her eyes when he finally broke the kiss. He leaned forward kissing each cheek and Carli realized she'd been crying. "Don't cry, *mon cher*. We'll always take care of your needs. Now, come for me."

Everything seemed to happen simultaneously. Tristan's fingers slid in curving forward to press firmly against the magic spot inside her. Lightning flashed through her entire body, throwing her over the edge of one of the most blindingly intense orgasms she'd ever experienced. Tristan barely caught her scream when he slammed his mouth over hers once again. Carli tried to lock her knees but it was no use, she felt them fold out from under her, but another pair of hands wrapped around her waist and she felt herself being pulled back against a chest so solid she knew immediately it was Parker. The heat from her core moved at the speed of light pushing out until even the tips of her fingers and toes felt like they were on fire. Wave after wave of pleasure coursed through her until she was completely spent.

"Jesus Christ she is beautiful when she comes. And the sweet cream flowing over my fingers makes me want to fuck her right here, right now."

"She certainly smells good enough to eat, and I'm looking forward to that more than I can tell you—but right now we have a problem." Carli heard the words, but her brain was still soaking in all those wonderful happy hormones and she wasn't quite ready to deal with anything labeled as a problem just yet. "Let's go, we need to get her cleaned up and ready to go. Cressida's been hurt." Hearing that her younger sister had been hurt was all it took to have her fighting back to the surface of awareness, but before she had a chance to protest, they were hustling her down a hallway to the opulent suite they'd been in earlier.

Carli had seen paramedics sprinting in the front door and quickly turned on her heel to follow, but Parker had simply scooped her up in his arms as if she weighed nothing at all and continued walking in the opposite direction. "Put me down you big lug." But the minute she struggled in earnest the balls inside her channel began to move and suddenly her body was reading from a different sheet of music than her brain. "I'm her family, she needs me. I need to be with her. I'm her next of kin for heaven's sake."

"No, princess, her husbands are with her and they're quite capable of taking care of all the legalities. I assure you Lawton and Brodie have crossed all those t's and dotted all the i's giving them the power to make decisions for their wife's health and well-being." His voice was surprisingly gentle but his arms were like steel bands—there would be no escaping his hold that was for sure. "I'll tell you everything I know as soon as we get in the suite. We'll get you cleaned up—and get those lovely little balls out of you, because I felt you stiffen when you moved and I know what they are doing to you."

By the time he'd set her on her feet in the master suite's bathroom, she was trembling and knew she didn't have a prayer of holding back the onslaught of tears. When she leaned against Parker's chest and let the first sob burst through, he simply wrapped her in the safety of his arms and let her cry.

Chapter Four

Parker needed to be working alongside his security detail, he knew they were in scramble-mode, but here he stood, holding a crashing submissive who'd just come apart in his arms moments before he'd told her that the younger sister she obviously adored had been hurt. She might argue whether or not she was a submissive, but that wouldn't change the fact it was true. He hadn't told her Cressida's injuries appeared to be serious because he'd suspected she would likely already be struggling with the emotional aftermath of the scene she'd just done with Tristan. There wasn't a Dom at The Knight's Club who wouldn't recognize an adrenaline crash when they saw one—and Carli Walker was in the deep end of one hell of a drop. Everything he'd learned about Carli told him that she'd pull herself together quickly, but for right now he was more than happy to simply hold her until the worst of the storm had blown over.

Tristan leaned against the wall after setting out everything she was going to need. He was ready to help her once she calmed, but at the moment Parker didn't see an ebb on the horizon. He knew she'd barely had time to take a breath since returning to the U.S., the woman was burning the candle at both ends and it appeared to be catching up with her. *If she belonged to us, we'd see to it that she took better care of herself.* Damn it, he had to stop thinking that way, Tristan would sniff his blood in the water in a heartbeat and the man was relentless when he wanted something—and Parker didn't have a doubt in the world his friend had set his sights on Carli Walker.

By the time she'd calmed enough for him to pull back, her make-up had all but disappeared and the woman beneath all the painted glitz was even more stunning than the one gracing magazine covers the world over. Most women looked horrible after an emotional venting like the one she'd just experienced, but Carli obviously hadn't gotten that memo because her face was mildly flushed and her eyes glassy with the remnants of her tears, but those were the only signs she'd just had a good cry. Thumbing the tears from her cheeks, he smiled down into eyes so bright green they were practically luminescent, "Better?"

"Yes, I think so. I'm sorry—really, I have no idea what that was about. It's embarrassing and I've eaten up valuable time with this nonsense." She was wrong to think she'd wasted anyone's time, this was emotion better vented here than someplace where they wouldn't be able to care for her properly—yet another thing she needed to learn.

"Princess, you needed that moment and we all know it. Don't shortchange yourself, your reaction didn't surprise or alarm either of us, and it shouldn't surprise you either. You've been keeping a killer schedule, and adding in an adrenaline crash along with disturbing news was a perfect recipe for this reaction." Pulling his phone from his chest pocket, he scanned his latest messages. "I'll be riding with you two to the hospital, but I need to get back out there. Here is what I know now, Cressida was shoved from the landing halfway up the stairway. She didn't fall all the way to the bottom, but everyone in the vicinity heard her head hit the marble. Their focus was on Cressida and no one caught up with her assailant. When EMS left with her a few minutes ago she was still unconscious. My team has reviewed the tape and whoever pushed her was wearing a mask similar to the ones you described earlier, and the footage doesn't have any sound, but one of my guys reads lips. Unfortunately that damned mask kept shifting and all he got was "for" and "sister" so we can only assume she was attacked either as a message to you or as a way to hurt you. In either case, we're not going to take any chances with your safety—you aren't to be out of either mine or Tristan's reach until told otherwise."

He could practically hear the thoughts racing through her mind, and he knew guilt was no doubt going to be chief among them. "Before you jump onto that runaway guilt train, stop and think about this logically. You had no way of knowing there was a threat to Cressida's safety. The fact this asshat caught her in one of the few moments her men didn't have a hand on her is nothing short of pure coincidence. Now, be a good girl and let Master Tristan help you clean up. I'll be ready to go in ten minutes, meet me out front." He didn't wait for a reply, he pressed a quick kiss to her forehead and then made his way back down the hall.

If he'd taken time to think about it, he wouldn't have been able to walk away from her, and for Carli *and* Cressida's sake he needed to focus on his job. The person who'd pushed Cressida had likely done so because Carli wasn't available—he intended to make sure she wasn't *ever* available again. He knew she had an upcoming trip and he mentally reviewed what it would take for both he and Tristan to clear their schedules to accompany her. It was something they'd have to figure out because he certainly didn't intend to let her go without at least one of them tagging along.

CARLI WAS LITERALLY bouncing in her seat by the time they reached the hospital. Parker had been getting updates as they drove and he'd kept her posted on her sister's condition, but nothing she'd heard made her feel any better. Rushing down the hall to the waiting room the nurse had pointed them to, she was relieved to find Lawton and Brodie both inside. But making her way across the room, she came to an abrupt halt when she saw the look on Lawton's face. Carli felt her whole body go cold causing her to begin shaking uncontrollably. Tristan wrapped his arm around her shoulders urging her forward, "Let's not borrow trouble, love. We need to hear what they have to say, jumping to conclusions is not going to help." He was right, but there was a small part of her that was afraid what she might learn was going to change her life forever—and she couldn't even begin to imagine the world without her sister in it. Deciding she couldn't let her fear win, Carli nodded her agreement and stepped up to where her two new brothers-in-law stood and asked, "How is she?"

Lawton's eyes were red and she could see he was struggling to remain composed, "We don't know much yet. I'm so sorry—I shouldn't have let her stay on the landing alone."

His pain was almost palatable and when she looked at Brodie she could see compassion in his eyes. The hard-nosed attorney with a reputation as a ruthless negotiator was obviously not holding his friend responsible for Cressida's injuries. Carli placed her hand over his forearm as she spoke, "Lawton, I don't believe for a minute you are responsible. The person who hurt Cressi was probably after me, so if anyone is to blame, it's me. I should have sought help when things felt *off*, but it never entered my mind she might be a target." He surprised her by pulling her into a rib-crushing hug and she was even more surprised at how much comfort she found in the gesture.

CRESSIDA COULD HEAR people all around her talking and there were strange beeping sounds that made her head feel like it was about to explode. Trying to sort through it all only made her head hurt worse so she stopped trying to figure out what was going on and why things felt so off-kilter. She floated in between conscious awareness and sleep for several more minutes before someone pulled her eyelid up and shined what had to have been a laser beam into her eyes. The explosion of pain that detonated in her head caused her to scream and that made her head hurt so bad she nearly threw up. Her instincts were to slap away the source of her pain, but a single voice broke through her frantic efforts to escape the light. Her new mother-in-law's voice sounded close to her ear, "Shhh, Cressi, I know it hurts, darling girl, but it's necessary. I promise we'll dim the lights as soon as we can." Soft, cool hands smoothed over her forehead and Cressi felt herself calming at Dr. Lana Hill's soothing touch.

"Hurts too much. Please. Where are Law and Brodie—I need them." Cressi was terrified that the only thing she'd been able to see when they'd opened her eyes was the blinding light, after the burn had faded everything else had been muted and blurred to the point even the people surrounding her were indistinguishable. The pain in her head was worse than anything she'd ever experienced and the only thing she could imagine easing her discomfort was being held by both of her husbands, and even in her befuddled state she knew that wasn't going to happen anytime soon so she did the next best thing—she pulled her mother-in-law close.

"Oh, sweetheart, I promise I'll bring those men of yours in here in just a few minutes. We've some more testing to do, but we're waiting on a few more people to arrive. I suspect those two men of yours are already precariously close to taking the waiting room apart. Now be a good girl and answer Dr. Bernstein's questions because he's still cranky that I woke him up to come in and look after you."

Cressida endured what felt like an interrogation, but refused to open her eyes because the pain wasn't abating at all. And since the neurologist hadn't demanded otherwise, she simply leaned back and kept her eyes tightly closed. She'd winced when the back of her head touched the pillow, and she felt someone slide a cold compress against what felt like an enormous bump. She wondered briefly what the man Lana had called Bernie looked like, because his voice was soft and pleasant. He also had a bit of a middle European accent, but the biggest thing was the strange sense of familiarity she felt listening to him—*odd that.*

Cressi didn't know how long she'd been sleeping, but as she started to surface the first thought that registered was the soothing feel of a hand sliding slowly up and down her arm—Lawton. Her other hand was being held between two warm hands as a thumb drew slow circles over the pulse point inside her wrist—a classic Brodie move. For the first time since before she'd realized she wasn't going to be able to regain her balance at the top of that staircase, she felt at peace.

"Pet, I know you are awake. Remember, no one knows you better than we do, so you might as well talk to us." She would have smiled if she hadn't been so afraid of moving, but she was floating in that strange zone between fully awake and asleep, so even though she'd heard his words, the full meaning was lost between synapses of nerve cells that were still not firing at full speed.

"Baby, the lights have been dimmed. You slept through a couple of the tests, but we need to see you open those lovely green eyes for us, sweetling." Cressi heard Lawton take a deep breath and then his voice changed as it took on a vulnerability that broke her heart. "Baby, please. I'm dying here, I need to know you are okay. I'm so sorry I couldn't get to you."

When Cressi heard Law's voice break, it was enough to pull her all the way to the surface of consciousness. She felt his fingers smooth over her brow before trailing down the side of her face and she forced herself to open her eyes. When her eyelids fluttered open she was relieved to see the lights were indeed very dim, in fact everything was so blurry she could barely make out their shapes. Panic set in, but when she fought to sit up the room started to spin and she dropped back against the pillow willing everything to settle before she was sick from the unnerving sensation of her world spinning.

"Pet, even I know you have to sit up very slowly after a concussion as severe as yours. Now—what I really want to know is what caused you to panic?"

"Blurry. Everything is so blurry. I can barely make out your shape, let alone see your face." The more she talked, the more hysterical she became making her head hurt even more, which caused her vision to become even more blurred. "We just got married...you shouldn't have to—"

"Stop. Stop right there, Cressida, because you are skating on very thin ice. Were you even listening to the vows we spoke to one another? Did you note the piece about in sickness and health? Because I was certainly listening, and when I made that vow to you, it meant something very significant to me."

Lawton's voice sounded from her other side, "Just as it did to me. I am surprised that you think so little of us, baby. Know this, sweet wife, we'll face whatever is to come together—all three of us." While she was relieved the sadness was gone from Lawton's voice, she wasn't at all happy that she'd disappointed them. But she couldn't imagine burdening them either even if she was convinced walking away would be the hardest thing she'd ever do in her entire life.

Before she could respond, Lana Hill's voice sounded from the side of her bed—God, she hadn't even seen her walk in the room. Her gasp of surprise gave away the fact she hadn't known the woman, who'd quickly become like a mother to her, was close and both men tightened their hold on her. "Glad to see you are awake, sweetheart, how do you feel? Give me a number for the pain in your head."

"Everything is blurry. I didn't even know you were here. How am I going to go to work Monday like this? And my head is going to explode, it's probably an eleven on a scale of one to ten." She hated venting, and she really hated admitting how badly her head hurt—but she was scared.

"Move over, darling, I want to be closer so Cressi can focus on my form." Lawton's hand slid away from her arm, but she immediately felt him settle his hand on top of her thigh. She loved the peaceful feeling her men brought with nothing more than a simple touch. Growing up with very little physical contact made her appreciate the intimacy created by their consistent contact even more. Lana gripped her forearm and leaned close until her form was easier to make out in the dim light. She also lowered her voice in volume and pitch, which eased the pounding in Cressi's head and she was grateful for her mother-in-law's insight and consideration. "Darling, the blurry vision is not a surprise...really, it's not a surprise at all. You've taken a severe blow to the back of the head and that means your sight is being compromised for two reasons. First of all, that horrible bruise at the back of your head is directly over the portion of your brain that controls sight, and secondly, brain swelling adversely affects the optic nerve as you can well imagine. Now, we don't know how long it will last, the time range is actually fairly broad, but I'll leave Bernie to explain all of that to you. What we are more concerned about right now is your level of pain, because that can be an indicator of a secondary problem, so we'll be doing everything we can to manage your discomfort without masking any of those other potential problems."

"Are you saying my sight might come back?"

"No. I'm saying your sight will very likely return to normal as soon as your body heals. Now, this is not my specialty—you know that, but I can assure you I have been calling everyone I know and your fathers-in-law are making similar calls. I snuck in to talk with you first because there are specialists already in the air on their way here—God, those two men can be downright diabolical in the way they manipulate people—although I must admit it's actually quite impressive when you aren't their target. Anyway, I wanted to ease your mind if I could because becoming upset will only aggravate your condition." Cressi wasn't entirely sure what her husbands' fathers had been up to, but their reputations in the business world spoke for itself. They were definitely men who were not easily deterred once they set their minds to something. If Lana said specialists were on their way, then they were—Cressi just wished she didn't need them.

CARLI WAS PRACTICALLY hyperventilating by the time Lawton reentered the waiting room to give them an update on Cressida's condition. When she heard that her sister's vision had been affected by the blow she'd taken to the back of the head, Carli had begun breathing so fast Tristan had been forced to pull her aside and calm her down. She didn't remember what he'd said, just that his presence had soothed her enough she'd finally been able to return to the group.

Lawton look stricken, it was easy to see he was heartsick and Carli's heart went out to him. She'd understood why he felt responsible for the fact his new wife had been injured, but there was no way he could have known the assailant would target her sister. "Listen, Carli, we are just grateful she's still with us. God knows how unforgiving marble is and she could have died so easily—I know I'll see that few seconds replayed in my nightmares for the rest of my life. The moment I realized I couldn't get to her in time was the worst in my entire life—Christ, we just made her ours and she could have so easily been taken from us."

Without hesitating, Carli wrapped her arms around her new brother-in-law, "Don't do this to yourself, Lawton. She's going to be all right, you said yourself the doctors think her vision will correct itself as she heals. Even if it doesn't, we've still got her and that's what's important." The instant she separated herself from Lawton, Parker wrapped his arm around her waist and pulled her back until she was snuggly fit against the steel muscles of chest. The move surprised her since she hadn't realized he'd moved from the other side of the room. She'd seen him standing near the floor to ceiling windows talking on the phone before Lawton had returned to the room. Looking up at Lawton, it was obvious he was surprised by the possessive move as well.

"Thanks, sweetie. I appreciate the hug even if it did set Parker on his ear." She realized Lawton's tone had lightened to something closer to teasing and she was thankful for Parker's distraction, even if she was confused by his method. *Why is he acting so possessive when I'm still not convinced he even likes me most of the time? Cripes, he is confusing—pick a side and stick with it, buddy.* Carli would use her next trip to sort through all her conflicting emotions—if she even got to go. She didn't have any intention of leaving until she knew everything was okay with her sister—luckily she had almost a week before she was supposed to be in London.

"When can I see her?" Carli wasn't sure she could rest until she had at least *seen* her younger sister, there was a lot of truth to the old saying "seeing is believing".

"We just got her to sleep and according to everyone we've talked to, that's the best thing for her at this point. They'll be waking her up periodically and she's going to be completely swamped with people in a few hours because Brodie's dad and my dad have pulled in people from all over the country." For the first time, Carli got a glimpse of the family her sister had married into and she felt her eyes fill with tears. "Sweetie? What's wrong?"

The concern in his voice caused Parker to release her, then turn her around so he could look down into her eyes, "Princess?"

"No—it's okay. I am just so happy Cressi's found the family she's always longed for—God knows she deserves it." Parker smiled down at her, the look so warm and genuine she couldn't help but stare at him. She hadn't realized until this moment that she hadn't actually seen that particular expression on his face before and it completely transformed his appearance. The only other time she'd seen him smile, she'd been across the room so she hadn't gotten the full effect. Holy hat racks, the man was handsome before, but when he smiled he looked like he belonged on the cover of GQ. *God in heaven the man is gorgeous...and hot!*

Parker's smile didn't waver, but the look in his eyes shifted from warm indulgence to molten sexuality before he leaned forward to whisper against her ear, "Princess, if you keep looking at me like that we'll be looking for a place to sate the hunger I see in your eyes before this conversation is over. And I'd rather the first time Master Tristan and I get you naked and between us, wasn't in a janitor's closet." Carli shuddered and then realized her entire body was leaning into Parker's as if she was being magnetically drawn to the steel conviction in his voice.

It took every ounce of willpower she could muster to look away from him and refocus her attention on Lawton. "Would it be alright if I just looked in on my sister? I promise I won't disturb her, I just need to *see* her." It didn't escape her attention that Lawton looked to Parker, who nodded so subtly she'd almost missed it.

"Okay, but I want you to promise you'll go back to

The Knight's Club with your men as soon as you've seen her. When she wakes up I want to be able to assure her you are in a safe place, and I know most of the security team is focused on Cressida right now so you'll be far safer there than here." *Her men? What was that supposed to mean?* She found herself following him and noted that Parker and Tristan flanked her on either side. When Lawton opened the door, she stepped just inside looking over to see Brodie sitting in a chair beside Cressi's bed holding her hand as she slept.

Seeing the slow rise and fall of her sister's chest made her sigh with relief and suddenly she felt completely spent. The hours she'd spent flying home, rushing to get ready for the party, and then everything that had taken place at the hotel—it was all starting to pile up on her and she was getting precariously close to completely shutting down. The thought had no sooner skittered through her mind than she felt Tristan's arm wrap around her waist, "Come on, *mon cher,* let's get you back home so you can rest—you are dead on your feet." Ordinarily Carli would have taken issue with being *handled*, at least in her personal life—but Tristan was right. She hadn't actually slept in a bed in three days, and the two-hours of fitful sleep she'd had on the last leg of her trip home hadn't done much to recharge her.

Carli knew she'd been burning the candle at both ends far too long—it was the reason she'd decided to scale back her schedule over the next several months. Her next trip would include a lot of downtime at both stops—something she intended to take full advantage of—that was, if her sister was well enough for her to leave. Shaking her head in an effort to clear the cobwebs quickly clouding her thinking, she simply nodded and turned to leave. As she stepped into the hallway, she saw Parker frowning at whatever he was reading on his phone, but Tristan quickly stepped between them before she could ask what was wrong.

She stumbled over the threshold at the hospital's entrance and before she could right herself, Tristan picked her up cradling her against his chest. *"Mon cher,* one of the first things we're going to teach you is that there is no shame in asking for our help. It angers us to see you struggle when we could so easily help you." Carli didn't have it in her to argue, she simply laid her head against his shoulder and closed her eyes, her last thought was how right it felt, but then she let herself slide into much needed sleep.

Chapter Five

TRISTAN SAT IN the back of the black SUV with Carli still in his arms. When he'd tried to settle her on the seat she grumbled, grabbing the front of his shirt and he hadn't had the heart to force the issue. Looking down he saw the contented look on her face as the vehicle's tinted windows muted the harsh light from the passing streetlamps. The softened light danced with the shadows that passed over her features in a continual play of light and shadows, and he was grateful the light wasn't disturbing her. The dark smudges under her eyes were shining through her porcelain skin where her make-up had been washed away by her tears. Those shadows were testaments to the depth of her fatigue, something he fully intended to see addressed in short order.

Had he not been watching her closely as they'd stepped from the hospital, she'd have gone ass over teakettle onto the sidewalk simply because she'd been too tired to lift her feet high enough to clear a small threshold at the door. After Tristan had settled with her in the backseat, Parker had shown him the message he'd received earlier and then climbed into the front passenger seat to make calls during the short drive to the club.

The woman Parker had sent to pick up a few things from Carli's apartment had found the door unlocked and the security system disabled. There didn't appear to be anything missing, but the large floral arrangement in the middle of the living room coffee table caught her attention because it had seemed out of place. There had been condensation on the outside of the cool vase indicating the arrangement had been fresh from a cooler when it was set on the small glass tabletop within the past hour or so. Parker gave the woman instructions before disconnecting the call and leaning back in his seat. Tristan wondered how much longer Parker was going to put off hiring the additional help he needed. Hell, he'd needed the extra people before both Carli's and Cressida's lives had been turned upside down by stalkers, and now he was definitely paying the piper for putting off the inevitable.

Tristan smiled to himself, one thing he knew about his friend was that his resistance to Carli Walker was a losing battle, the chemistry between them was too strong. Parker might think he could compartmentalize his feelings when it came to women—and in truth he'd been quite successful up until now. But the woman curled in Tristan's lap like a contented kitten, was going to challenge Parker Daniels on every level—her fire was exactly what Parker needed. But it was the soft, vulnerable side of Carli Walker that called to Tristan. He'd wrap her in cotton batting and be her shelter in every storm if she'd let him. Stroking the tips of his fingers along her jawline, he smiled when she snuggled closer and sighed. Carli's soul already recognized him as her safe haven—all he needed to do was bring that sharp mind of hers on board.

They were only a few blocks from the club when he felt his phone vibrating in his pocket. Tristan was surprised to see a message from the man sitting in the front seat. *CW's itinerary for upcoming trip. What is your schedule like?*

We'll confer. Opening the attachment, Tristan smiled when he saw Carli would be in London for ten days with very little of that time devoted to work. His parents were going to be over the moon that he and Parker had finally found her. He quickly skimmed the rest of her schedule and was pleased to see a week in Rio listed as well. Both stops would give her time to rejuvenate if she had them with her to help manage the demands for her time—which he suspected tended to snowball on her.

The logistics alone for her travel must be a monumental task and Tristan wondered about the staff assisting her—did she consider them her friends? She'd mentioned last evening that she was concerned the person responsible for the masks was a part of her inner circle and how frightened she was by the thought. Considering how much time she spent with the entourage traveling with her, he wasn't surprised by her concern. Before he closed the program on his phone he sent it to both his home and his office printers, he preferred looking at hard copies when discussing plans with the other Knights of the Boardroom as they'd been affectionately labeled by the media, there was nothing like pen and paper to solidify plans.

The four of them had laughed when they'd first heard the media moniker, but they'd also seen it as a great marketing strategy and capitalized on it. Their commitment to honor when dealing with clients and Templar's financial support of a plethora of charities had added fuel the comparisons. But they'd sealed the deal when they'd incorporated their own version of The Knight's Code into the club's charter. Local reporters had tried every trick in the book to make their way inside The Knight's Club— even before it officially opened, but none had managed to slip through Parker's security, something Tristan found damned impressive. However, the reporters' lack of first-hand information hadn't kept them from speculating, and as always, there wasn't more than a grain of truth to what they'd printed.

Their driver parked in the more private area behind the club and before they'd even entered the elevator, Parker's phone signaled an incoming message. Tapping furiously as he muttered something about, "Fucking flowers," Tristan watched as Parker pressed send and then looked up at the sleeping woman in his arms. "Good God, she's an even bigger trouble magnet than her sister. There was another flower delivery a few minutes ago—here. Lots of sweet little gizmos in this one too—Curt's going to think he's died and gone to heaven getting all those little jewels. Really glad our scramblers were working since it sat on the front desk for an hour during check-in before anybody had time to move it—looks like I'm not the only one who needs to hire more help."

Tristan nodded in agreement, he'd known he would need to enlarge his staff when they found a woman of their own, but he hadn't expected to need them on board quite this quickly. He'd begun screening applicants since his friends married Cressida because he'd seen that as a sign they'd find their own woman soon—little had he known how right he was. Several of his best applicants were already club members, and he'd be making those calls sooner rather than later.

PARKER WAS AT his wits end—he prided himself on being good at anticipating and preempting problems, but the last few weeks had been a fast downward spiral and the last eighteen hours were as close to a complete clusterfuck as he'd ever dealt with. Jesus, Joseph, and Mary, who knew two women could attract so much trouble without even trying? He'd given his second in command *carte blanche* to handle things for the next several hours and Parker turned his phone off. He needed the down time and Carli deserved some of his undivided attention—hell, every time he'd started to make a connection with her they'd been interrupted.

When the doors of the elevator opened into Tristan's home, they made their way quickly to the master suite bathroom. Getting Carli awake enough to stand proved to be difficult to say the least—and amusing, too. Parker had heard about people who appeared drunk when they were just exhausted, but he'd never actually dealt with one until now. When he tried to slip the straps of her dress off her shoulders, Carli giggled and slapped at his hands, "Hey, you need to ask nice if you want to see what's behind the two curtains in the middle."

Tristan's snort of laughter had Carli turning so quickly in his direction she actually fell into his chest. *"Mon cher,* under ordinary circumstances slapping the hands of one of your Doms when he is trying to undress you would earn you a session over a spanking bench you wouldn't enjoy much. But I think we're going to let that one pass with a warning since I'm fairly sure you aren't behaving as you normally would." *Yeah, Harris—there's an understatement of monumental proportions.*

"What? Am I being a bad girl? Whatcha gonna do about that, gorgeous?" Parker wanted to laugh at the way Tristan's nostrils flared at her words—oh yeah, the Big Kahuna of The Knight's Club wasn't used to being challenged by a sub, this evening just gets more interesting by the minute. "Wow, did you know there's steam coming out of your ears? That's pretty amazing."

Parker figured since he was technically responsible for her personal safety, it was probably time to intervene. "Princess, you really need to stop talking. Come on, let's get you in the shower, hopefully the water will pull you out of this punch-drunk stupor you're in before Master Tristan warms your backside." He stripped her and then himself in the time it took Tristan to rid himself of his own clothes. Parker knew his friend was trying to give him the reins for a while since he and Carli had spent more time together, it was time for Parker to play catch up.

Carli was in front of him, completely bare for the first time, and Parker couldn't take his eyes off her. He hadn't actually stood next to her when she wasn't wearing those damned four inch heels she seemed to favor, so he hadn't realized how truly petite she was. At six foot four he towered over her, and that wasn't even taking into account their body frames. He'd been a collegiate linebacker, and for the first time he was actually worried his body size might intimidate the woman he planned to fuck.

"Come on, beautiful, let's get in the shower before I decide I can't wait that long."

Carli looked up at him, her eyes clearer than they had been just a few seconds before, "You didn't call me princess. Are you mad at me?"

What?

"Not at all, why would you think that?" He led her into the shower—which was actually a small glass-enclosed room. The longest wall looked out over the building's atrium and the effect was pretty incredible.

When she realized the wall was essentially a window, she gasped and stepped back so quickly she slipped, but

Tristan caught her once again. Parker could see his friend had definitely shifted gears and he leaned back to watch. *"Mon cher*, that is twice in less than an hour I've caught you, so I hope you are noticing a pattern. When you fall, we'll always catch you. Why were you trying to get away from the wall?"

"Holy shit, I can see people milling," the sharp crack of a hand hitting bare flesh echoed through the small enclosure and Parker didn't even try to hide his smile. "Hey, what the hell was that," another smack sounded as Tristan's hand connected again with Carli's ass. He'd interrupted her once again and Parker wondered how many times she was going to curse before she figured it out. "Now just a damned minute." When the third swat landed, she turned to him with big tears in her eyes and he knew she hadn't been hurt, Parker recognized tears of confusion when he saw them.

"Princess, watch your language. Unfortunately you are pressing one of his hot buttons. And I know you are aware of the no cursing rule because you were warned last night." He saw the flair of recognition in her eyes, but it morphed into need so quickly he had to blink to be sure his observation wasn't wishful thinking. *Nope, a naughty girl is in there, one who is going to push us to the very edge so we'll prove ourselves worthy—well, bring your best game, princess, batter up.* Turning her so her breasts were pressing against the cool glass, he used the entire expanse of his large hand to slowly caress a path from the base of her skull to the very bottom of her spine.

God he loved the little dimples sitting so pretty on the very top curve of her ass cheeks. "If you belonged to us, we'd enjoy showing you off, princess. We'd keep you naked most of the time when were alone so every delectable inch of you was available to our every whim and fancy. Displaying you in the club would be fun, too—although neither of us has ever been particularly fond of sharing with anyone else." Focusing most of the pressure on his middle finger, Parker slid his hand down over the sweet curves of her ass letting his longest finger part the wet globes. "The people you see down in the open area are in The Knight's Club, princess. At this time of the morning, I can assure you those are employees and they are completely focused on their jobs. But rest assure, each and every one of them has been thoroughly vetted. They've all worked a variety of shifts, so seeing a beautiful woman naked is not newsworthy."

He'd been stroking his finger slowly up and back along her folds as he'd been speaking and she had not only relaxed in his hold, but she'd pressed herself tighter against the glass. God Almighty how he'd love to get a look at her from his bedroom window. "Look directly across from us and down one floor, baby. See the windows where the draperies are open?" There wasn't a doubt in his mind, Carli Walker was an exhibitionist—hell, the fact she was a model almost guaranteed it on at least some level. He also suspected they'd have to be very careful, because if his hunch was right, parading her around naked in the main areas of the club wasn't going to work for her.

"Yes," the word was practically a moan, but Parker was pleased that she'd actually answered rather than simply nodded her head.

"That large bed you see? It belongs to me. Do you understand what that means, princess?" This time he didn't wait for an answer, he slid two fingers in deep, swirling them around—testing her. Either she hadn't had sex in a long time or she was spending time with someone a lot smaller than either of the two men she was standing between now. "That means when you are spending time alone with one of us, you'll be able to share a bit of the fun. Master Tristan can fuck you up against this window and I'll lay in my bed and watch. I'll know when you climax by the look on your face. And Master Tristan will have a front row seat while I've got you tied to my bed, brining you right to the edge of release time and time again until you're begging me to let you come."

Parker punctuated his last words by pressing against her G-spot and she detonated in his arms. Her scream echoed off the walls followed by his and Tristan's moans of frustration. He'd wanted to be deep inside her the first time he made her come, but she needed to be loosened up or they were going to hurt her. Using her endorphin-fueled euphoria to his advantage, Parker asked, "How long has it been since you've had sex, Carli?"

He pulled her back against his chest and turned so she faced Tristan. His friend's puzzled look made him grin as he mouthed *very tight* over her head. Tristan's eyes widened infinitesimally. Since she'd been wearing the balls earlier, Parker knew his friend hadn't pushed deep enough to make the discovery. *Yeah, I would have assumed Ms. Walker was sexually active, too. But her body tells a different tale.*

"Mon cher, Master Parker's question is not a difficult one, and I can assure you he has a very good reason for asking." Tristan stepped forward to cup the side of Carli's face in his palm, smoothing his fingers over her lower lip. Parker felt Carli's shoulders drop and would have assumed she'd simply relaxed at Tristan's touch, but the rest of her body was practically vibrating with tension. He'd also noticed she was taking deep breaths for no apparent reason, and wondered why. Apparently the change in her breathing hadn't escaped Tristan's attention—no big surprise there. "Love, I train in a wide variety of martial arts disciplines, so I'm well versed in the various ways deep breathing can be utilized. Since you are nearing physical exhaustion, I suspect you're using it to flood your brain with oxygen hoping it will help you navigate this conversation."

Now it was Parker's turn to be surprised. He'd never topped a woman who'd done this particular breathing exercise on her own. Parker and Tristan had used it with subs who were having trouble coming all the way out of sub-space—but having their sweet sub use the technique herself, just to talk to them, was something entirely new. He'd poured over her background information when he'd first been hired by her modeling agency to protect her, and it had been easy to see the woman was far more than a pretty face. She graduated at the top of her class in both her undergraduate and MBA programs.

Carli Walker had shown an amazing aptitude for the stock market and had made a ton of money in the past few years. Since the markets weren't his area of expertise, he'd asked Law's dad to take a look, hoping there might be a clue there as to who was stalking her. And even though he hadn't seen anything troubling, Patrick Hill had been more than a little impressed. He'd called Carli's diversification forward thinking brilliance and one of New York's wealthiest financial gurus had actually whistled as he'd looked over the summaries. "I want to hire her—yesterday. She's never actually worked for a brokerage or any other financial institution as far as I can see and she's anticipated moves seasoned traders missed. I mean what I said—I'd hire her in a heartbeat even though I typically avoid hiring family members, even extended ones. But if any of my competition get wind of this—they'll hound the girl to death, which is why I suspect she's keeping her profitable record under wraps."

"Four years." Carli's voice had been so quiet he'd barely heard her, but even as quiet as they'd been the words packed a hell of a punch. For the first time in years Parker was grateful a sub hadn't been able to see his expression because he knew he hadn't masked his surprise—thank God Tristan had remained stoic. The man had simply nodded and stepped to the side and pulled her under the spray. Parker could hear Tristan speaking softly to her as he washed and then conditioned her hair, but he wasn't focused on anything but his shock at her answer.

Shaking off his wayward thoughts, he quickly finished his own shower and led Carli into the open space of the bathroom while Tristan finished cleaning up. By the time he'd dried both of them, Tristan stepped out and grabbed the last towel from the warming rack. "I'm going to get us all a glass of wine—and yes, I know full well what time it is, but our bodies are still functioning as if it were late evening. And I believe the coming discussion will be easier if we are relaxed." Parker certainly wasn't going to argue the point even though he didn't ordinarily drink wine. He still preferred ice-cold beer, it was one of the few Texas habits he hadn't shaken when he moved to the northeastern part of the country.

By the time they'd settled Carli in a chair in the living room, she'd already downed the glass of wine Tristan had poured for her. His raised brow brought a nice flush to her cheeks and Parker laughed as he traded glasses with her and headed to the bar to pull a bottle of beer from the fridge. "Here, princess, this works out well for me anyway." When he returned most of that glass was gone as well and her cheeks were already turning a lovely shade of pink. *Perfect.*

Chapter Six

CARLI WAS ALREADY feeling the effects of the wine as Parker settled into a chair across from her. There were three different conversation groupings in the massive living room and she knew they'd deliberately chosen the most intimate of the three. The chairs were comfortably upholstered wingbacks that made her feel as if she was being hugged from behind. Thinking about a piece of furniture displaying emotion was ridiculous, but she found herself giggling anyway. *Yeah, probably should have had a glass of water first, dumbass. Wow! Did Tristan just growl at me?*

Meeting his gaze, Carli saw a whole different kind of heat. She hadn't had so much to drink that she couldn't pick out the pissed off man in the room. "That's five. You've already been warned about your language, now I'm warning you about self-depreciating remarks. While it's convenient for us that you randomly speak your thoughts out loud, I'm fairly certain it's a habit you'll want to break—soon."

"Personally, I hope she's a slow learner. I think I'm going to enjoy seeing that fine ass bared and draped over my lap—or the bed—or a spanking bench. Hell, I'll enjoy seeing it pretty much everywhere I can think of." She was surprised that Parker had been the one to lighten the moment, she was beginning to think she'd pegged the wrong man as the stricter of the two. "Let's get this chat behind us so we can move on to something more fun. We're all tired, but none of us are going to really rest until we've addressed a few things. First of all, please tell me why you haven't had sex in so long, because, princess, I'm never going to believe it's because you haven't had ample opportunities."

WOMEN AS SMART and beautiful as Carli Walker almost always had more offers than they wanted, so Parker knew it was her choice—he just didn't know why she'd made it. He watched as she took a deep breath and swirled what little wine was left in her glass slowly around the inside of the crystal with practiced ease, "I've tried to keep myself busy—school, then juggling two careers." She gave him a pointed look, "Don't even try to deny knowing about my investments because you pinged every single digital trip wire I'd set up when you did my background check. I can help you avoid that pitfall in the future if you want..."

Holy fucking shit, he hadn't seen that one coming and Tristan's bark of laughter meant his expression had given him away. Goddammit to hell, he was going to have to completely rethink his protocol if she'd known about the checks.

"Talk about your Kodak moment. Hire her as a consultant so you don't get hung up in that damned nepotism clause we thought was such a great idea—but for God's sake hire the woman." Tristan's laughter relaxed the tension in the room and when he finally laughed at himself, Carli seemed to relax as well.

"Anyway, the few times I had sex it just didn't—well, it

didn't seem to live up to all the hype, so I didn't think I was really giving up that much." Parker knew her words were probably only half the story, but he wasn't going to call her on it—at least not yet. Evidently she hadn't found what she was looking for and being under such public scrutiny would have made searching very difficult, not to mention monumentally embarrassing when she was exposed and in today's world, eventual exposure was a given. The wrinkles between Tristan's brows let Parker know the other Dom hadn't missed her lie—although he honestly felt she was probably lying to herself as well. It was going to be fun to show her what she'd been missing.

Parker watched as she took another deep breath and then gulped down the last of the wine in her glass before speaking again, "I'm fairly sure the next item on the agenda is birth control, so I'll skip the preliminaries because I am equally sure you already know the answer. Yes I'm covered—not for the reason you think, but there it is. And I'm clean—not that I probably needed to mention that part all things considered. But Cressi said her men weren't big fans of condoms...so I just figured... Anyway, I don't do well with latex." That had also been in her medical file, but Parker didn't see any reason to add insult to injury when she was already uncomfortable with everything they already knew about her.

CARLI HADN'T EVEN realized she'd dropped her gaze to the floor in front of her until she heard Tristan's command, "Look at me, *mon cher*." This time she didn't solely react to the words, but made a conscious choice to lift her gaze to meet his. His quick nod acknowledged the fact he'd seen the difference, "Ordinarily we'd never play with a submissive without doing all the paperwork first. I've printed out our latest blood screens for you, they are laying on the bar if you'd like to see them. But I want you to know, we don't consider what's going to happen a scene in the traditional sense—we want you, it's just that simple. All of that aside, nothing—and I mean nothing happens that you don't want to happen. You said you'd read up on the lifestyle so you should already have learned our guiding tenants are safe, sane, and consensual."

"If you haven't already done so, princess—commit that expression to memory. Those three words will always guide everything between us—kink or vanilla." Parker was watching her closely for a response and Carli wanted them to know she understood, but she couldn't get the words past the lump in her throat, so she hoped her eyes conveyed how grateful she was they were being cautious with her. "Tell us what you expect from us, princess."

Carli was certain her face had given away her surprise so she didn't even try to hide it, "Oh, well, I don't really know how to answer that. I guess I thought you wanted to have sex with me. That was probably presumptuous of me. It's okay, really." She felt her face heat with embarrassment and she blinked back the tears that had filled her eyes. *I will not cry!*

Unfolding her legs from where she'd tucked them beneath her, she'd barely managed to stand when Parker's voice sounded from inches in front of her. How he'd managed to close the distance between them so quickly without her even seeing him move she had no idea—after all, he was a really big man for Pete's sake. "Where do you think you are going, princess?" She really hadn't had a plan, she just wanted to end this humiliating conversation as quickly as possible. "Come." He grabbed her hand and led her back to the chair he'd just vacated. Settling her on his lap so she faced Tristan, Parker broke the silence after several long seconds, "Don't ever walk away from your Doms during a conversation, princess—that particular offense is right up there with lying, and it's on the short list of things you'll want to avoid at all costs."

"And let's clarify—lying includes lying by omission." Tristan's expression was stern, but he didn't look angry at her, just completely focused. "When we inquired about what you expected, we simply wanted to know how you saw tonight playing out. If—and I do mean IF we don't want to have sex with you, we'll explain that to you. We may be tired or we may feel you are too tired—but rest assured we'll explain so you don't ever assume it's because we don't want you, *mon cher.*"

Carli felt tears fill her eyes once again, but for an entirely different reason. Parker rubbed soothing circles over her lower back and that small gesture calmed her more than she'd expected it to. She heard him sigh and when she looked up at him, his expression could only be described as regretful. "Let's leave that question open for a minute, princess. First, I want to tell you what I learned while you were sleeping in the car. Someone broke into your apartment." Carli felt her entire body react and the fear that swept through her made the room spin around her, making it seem as though she was standing in the center of a carrousel ride.

Looking down, she realized Tristan was kneeling in front of her with her cradling between his palms, "Breathe with me, Carli. You know how to do this, I've seen you focus with deep breathing." He was right, getting some much-needed oxygen into her system was the only thing that would stem the dizziness, and she worked to sync her breathing with his. When she felt settled, she simply nodded, he pressed a chaste kiss to the center of her forehead, "Good girl." She felt herself warm at his words, but before she had a chance to wonder about it, Carli remembered what had sent her into a panic.

"Templar's security team is taking care of the details with the police tonight, but you'll need to do a more thorough look around tomorrow when you pack."

Carli blinked up at him in surprise, "Pack? I'm not even sure I'll be going on the next photo shoot, a lot of that trip was downtime anyway. I can't leave with Cressida in the hospital."

Parker's hand had once again begun the slow, soothing circles over the sensitive spot at the base of her spine. She wasn't sure he knew the full effect that simple touch was having, but as perceptive as the two of them seemed to be, it was likely. "Princess, we know how important your sister is to you. I wasn't talking about packing for the trip—although, I do believe you'll decide to go because I think she'll be well on her way to recovery before then."

"*Mon cher*, Master Parker and I would like for you to stay here until we all agree it's safe for you to return to your apartment. We'll discuss all the details later, but for tonight we wanted you to know about the break in."

"When I said there hadn't been anything taken, I didn't mean to imply there wasn't evidence. There was a floral arrangement left on your coffee table and it contained several different recording devices. Again, we'll get more information tomorrow, but neither of us would have felt right about proceeding without telling you what we knew." Parker's words made her realize they'd taken a huge risk interrupting their plans to make sure she was up to date on what had happened. Rather than derailing their plans, it made her appreciate them even more. She wasn't entirely sure staying with them here was a good idea, but the truth was she didn't really have anywhere else to go.

Staying at Cressi's was out because her sister and her husbands already had enough on their plates, and she wasn't close to anyone besides Phillip, and his active social life meant she'd be alone most of the time there as well. She hadn't felt safe at her apartment prior to the break in and she'd be terrified living there alone now, so their offer to stay with them really was the best option. Carli would just have to make a concentrated effort to remember they were simply helping her explore her sexuality—their reputations as playboy bachelors had been well documented in the media and she didn't harbor any illusions she'd be enough to change their minds.

Realizing they were waiting for her to respond, Carli nodded, "Thank you, I appreciate your offer, I'll try to not overstay my welcome." She didn't miss the creases that formed briefly between Tristan's brows or the slight hesitance in Parker's touch despite the fact her body was swinging wildly between physical exhaustion and sexual arousal.

Just as she decided to move, Parker stood keeping her in his arms and started walking back down the hall. "Enough talking. Do you want to see the paperwork, princess?"

She shook her head, "No. I trust you. I wouldn't be here if I didn't trust you both." And for the first time since her mother died, Carli realized she didn't feel like she had to face down what was to come alone. The strange sense of peace that washed over her was a pleasant surprise, she'd try to live in the moment—at least for the next few hours. *She deserved this after the past couple of days.* That was her story and she was going to stick to it.

LOOKING DOWN ON his bed, seeing Carli laid out in front of him like a beautiful offering made Tristan's heart skip a couple of beats. While it was true she was stunningly gorgeous—hell, that was something the entire world knew. But it wasn't her physical beauty that drew him to her like a magnet to steel; it was the soul he saw reflected in her brilliant green eyes. Each time he looked into her eyes he swore they were a different variation of green. He'd seen them so bright they reminded him of the lush countryside north of London—the fields surrounding his parents' home were almost alive with the brightest shades of green. But right now, Carli's eyes were a much deeper hue—more emerald in color. A vision of her wearing a diamond and emerald collar moved through his mind so clearly, Tristan knew in that moment he'd been given a glimpse into their future.

"*Mon cher*, tonight is about pleasure. It's about the two of us learning what you enjoy and exploiting it until you are screaming our names as you come." She'd said her sexual experience had failed to live up to the hype so it hadn't seemed like she was giving up much—they would show her the *hype* had probably actually set the bar too low. He'd heard submissives make similar comments time and again during their interviews at the club. Those same subs were the ones who became the most devoted club members, because they were finally able to find the fulfillment that had eluded them for years. "Repeat the safe words and when you are supposed to use them for me, please." Even though he'd decided to hold over the five swats she'd earned, he still wanted her to know safe words would always apply. Over time they would know her better than she knew herself and it wouldn't be something they needed to review regularly—but until then, both he and Parker would remind her often.

"Red for stop, yellow for pause, and green for go. Are you still mad at me for cursing?" Tristan knew she wasn't really that concerned about the swats, it was entirely possible the anticipation of them and the knowledge she'd disappointed him would go further to correct her behavior—time would tell.

"I wasn't angry. I was disappointed because you are better than that, *mon cher*. Rest assured you'll get those swats, but not tonight. We want to play with you, we want to show you that your expectations can be far exceeded by our reality." He'd been moving slowly into position as he'd been speaking and Parker had done the same. Tristan nudged her legs apart, "Show me, baby. I want to look at you. There won't be a square inch of your delectable body we won't know intimately—shyness has no place between us." Carli's eyes never left his, but they were clouding beautifully with lust—a look every Dom he knew responded to.

Parker was sitting closer to the headboard, "Give me your wrists, princess." Both Tristan and Parker loved bondage—all forms of bondage, excluding anything related to breath play, which they still didn't allow anywhere in the club for obvious safety reasons. Tristan knew Parker was about to give their woman a small taste of bondage—they'd be able to judge her reaction and know how to proceed with her. What she wouldn't realize for a while was that everything they did was with the next step in mind. They would begin as they intended to go because the goal would be to help her explore anything she found intriguing, subject to their mutual hard limits.

Carli had only hesitated a second before raising her arms to place her wrists in Parker's huge hands, they'd teased him for years about the size of his hands. Parker Daniels was a big man—everywhere. Tristan was considered large, but his cock wasn't as broad as Parker's so he would be the first to make love to Carli. It wasn't usually an issue because they played with experienced and sexually active submissives, but as soon as they'd discovered how long it had been for her, Plan B had gone into effect.

Tristan used the pads of his fingers smoothing them down the sensitive crease between the top of her thigh and her sex causing her legs to jerk. He knew the reaction was more reflex than a genuine attempt to close her legs, but he addressed it anyway, "None of that, *mon cher*. You must hold still—if you cannot do that, I'll be happy to wrap something silky around your knees and tie them open, that would check one thing off my bucket list right away. Tying you to my bed is pretty high on that list, you know." And there was the reaction he'd hoped for: her eyes dilated, her breathing hitched perfectly, and the warm blush moving up her chest was gorgeous. But the rush of her honey, which was now trickling down the quivering folds of her labia in sparkling rivulets, was the hottest thing he'd ever seen. He'd be willing to bet he could talk her over the edge of orgasm, and given the opportunity, he was looking forward to testing the theory.

Parker had wrapped a beautiful piece of silk around her wrists in a delicate pattern that looked more like an accessory than a binding and Tristan wanted to laugh at the surprised look on Carli's face when he'd finished.

Don't worry, love—you're going to understand soon enough. See that tail at the end? That's been left for a reason.

Chapter Seven

CARLI KNEW HER mind wasn't processing everything as individual pieces of the larger picture the way she ordinarily did—the ability to see patterns in events had always been the thing that allowed her to make accurate predictions about what was to come in the markets. Many of her on-line business contacts had ask her where she got her information, but she'd never been able to explain it...not that she'd given it much effort. How did you explain to someone what you saw so clearly in your mind's eye if they couldn't see it too? She'd been accused of being everything from psychic to criminal, but no one was as meticulous about record keeping as she was so her innocence would always be easy to prove. And as for being psychic—she could only wish it was that easy. No, her business acumen was the result of hours and hours of painstaking research, not some magical, mystical insight.

Tristan seemed to sense her need for predictability in order to maintain control and he was absolutely diabolical in his ability to rain chaos down upon her. The first orgasm had hit so hard and fast she'd been completely unprepared for it. He'd been talking to her—just talking to her for God's sake, and then she'd looked at the intricate pattern of silk Parker had used to bind her wrists together—but then several things happened at the same time and the explosion of light behind her eyes had been spectacular. The ball of heat that burst from the deepest part of her core reached all the way to her toes and the tips of her fingers—hell, everything was still tingling. When he'd set his mouth over the top of her sex and growled, *"Mine!"* she hadn't been able to hold back her own reaction.

"God in heaven you taste positively divine, *mon cher.* Your honey is as sweet as the juice of a ripe peach, and I'm looking forward to spending hours tracing each sweet fold of your pussy. The smooth surface of your skin is addictive, the soft petals of your sex are swollen and flushed the deepest rose color I've ever seen, reminding me why the knights of the realm loved using dark red roses as their symbol for love. Painting roses on their vestments gave them inspiration—it was their way of remembering what they were fighting for, what awaited them at home." All the time he'd been speaking, Tristan had been moving up her body, pressing soft kisses along a path up her torso until she felt the tip of his penis pressing against her opening. "I want you. I'm going to be so deep inside you I'll be able to feel your heart beating. I'll feel each breath you take, and I'll feel each ripple of your pussy as I push you further and further toward the edge of reason."

There were several seconds of silence, Carli suspected they were giving her a chance to process everything Tristan had just said—part of The Knight's Club's commitment to ensuring the sex was consensual no doubt. She'd read their website from start to finish—more than once, and been impressed with how many times and ways she'd seen that recurring theme. They must have seen something in her expression that assured them she was focused enough to actually give her consent, because Parker started to move her bound hands over her head.

"See this tail, princess?" He held up a length of silk that she'd simply thought had been left over from the binding he'd done on her wrists—but perhaps not.

"Yes." Parker didn't continue, he just raised a brow and waited. It took her a few seconds, but she finally realized what he was waiting for and amended her answer, "Yes, sir."

"I like the way that sounds, and I'm willing to wait for you to call me Master. But rest assured, princess, that is exactly where we're headed. Straighten your arms and grasp the headboard, baby." Carli had noticed the intricate metalwork of the headboard the night she'd been looking for Cressi and tried—unsuccessfully—to enter The Knight's Club. Looking back on that now, she was more than a little embarrassed by her behavior. All things considered, she should probably be grateful they hadn't called the police, she'd been running on fear and fumes—always a bad combination.

"*Mon cher*, you need to stay with us. Letting your mind wander when you are with your Doms is not in your best interest. Now, answer Master Parker's question before we are forced to rethink our plans to keep this all about pleasure." *Question? Oh shit, I didn't even hear a question.*

Deciding honesty was her only choice, Carli shifted her attention to Parker, "I'm sorry. He's right, my mind was wandering. I was just thinking about the first night I came to the club looking for Cressida, and now...looking back on the way I behaved, I'm grateful you didn't call the police." His eyes softened and the tiny lines at the corners of his eyes that had let her know how frustrated he'd been smoothed out making him look even more devastatingly handsome. "Can you repeat the question, please?"

Parker gave her a small grin and nodded, "Your honesty and openness has saved you, princess—well done. I asked if you'd ever been bound before."

"No, I haven't—wait, I was...well, sort of, for a shoot once." It had been before she had an agency representing her and those damned pictures still haunted her. She hadn't been nude, but the bikini they'd given her was so microscopic there certainly hadn't been much of her left to anyone's imagination. "But, it was a long time ago, and I certainly wouldn't want to judge anything by that experience." Both men we looking at her with glacial expressions and she realized how poorly she'd explained herself, "It wasn't what you are thinking. It was just cheesy and embarrassing. Nothing that will hit the news and embarrass you—much." *I hope.*

"We weren't worried about our reputations, princess. I do believe that ship has sailed. We will be having a discussion about this someday, but for now, knowing you won't have a flashback is good enough." *Flashback? Going to have to Google that one.*

PARKER COULD TELL Carli hadn't understood what he'd meant, but from what he'd learned about her, he also suspected, at her next opportunity, she'd be researching the subject. From all appearances, the woman had a serious information addiction. He'd also be looking for the pictures she'd mentioned, no need for her to worry about those floating around, and it was easy to see she was worried they might pop-up despite her claim to the contrary. It was also the first chink he'd seen in her reputation for only taking modeling jobs for a short list of companies. Carli Walker had a reputation for integrity, so any deviation from that might give them a clue as to who was targeting her.

"While Master Tristan is fucking that sweet pussy of yours, I'm going to enjoy your mouth." Her eyes flared with a brief panic before she masked it and he knew then her minimal sexual experience wasn't limited simply to vaginal intercourse. When he finished securing the pull-away knot, he held the last length of silk in his hand, "Open your hand, princess." When she did, he laid the silk along her palm. "Since you are new to bondage and we haven't played together before, it's important for you to have a tangible reminder that you are in charge—*always*. Tugging on this will release the knot and your hands from the headboard, but if we are doing our jobs right, you'll be enjoying yourself too much to worry about it."

Hoping his grin conveyed how much he was looking forward to their time together, he leaned down and pressed a quick kiss against her lips when she snaked her tongue out in obvious anticipation. "Princess, I've been looking forward to this since the first time I saw you. Let's play." Tristan recognized his cue and pressed forward, sinking his cock into her wet pussy. Parker knew his friend had been slowly stretching her as he'd been explaining their plan, but the suddenness of Tristan's movement caused her to gasp in surprise; it was the moment he'd been waiting for and Parker didn't hesitate to take advantage. The tables were quickly turned, because the moment moist heat surrounded the head of his cock, Parker's head dropped back on his shoulders, a loud moan vibrating from deep in his chest. "Goddamn, princess. Your mouth is like liquid fire."

She sucked him in further and for several seconds Parker was forced to let her take control because he was too lost in pleasure to fight her. "*Mon cher,* I do believe you've rendered him speechless and I don't think I've ever seen that happen before." Tristan's words were enough to pull him back from the edge, and he appreciated his friend's insight. Parker couldn't remember the last time he'd been so close to letting a woman take the reins during a scene.

Reminding himself that he wasn't ready to settle down yet was becoming increasingly difficult as the *rightness* of the moment washed over him. And while he still was far from convinced this was the way he wanted to spend the rest of his life, he also could no longer ignore the fact things felt different with Carli.

Parker set a pace that matched the one Tristan was using in his thrusts so one of them was filling her at all times. But neither of them was going to last long, hell, her mouth was lethal. His release blindsided him and before he'd even had a chance to warn her, Parker felt the first pulses as he shot his seed down her throat. She swallowed quickly, barely losing any of what he'd given her. Parker had barely pulled from her hot little mouth before her entire body arched and he was sure he'd seen Tristan stiffen and call out her name before collapsing down onto her, then rolling to the side.

Once he caught his breath and his eyes could focus again, Parker looked down at the woman who had just shattered his control and blown all the pieces into another dimension, he was surprised to see she was looking at him thoughtfully. "Is it always like that?" He watched her eyes shift to Tristan before adding, "I mean, is that the way it's supposed to be? Because, well...I have to tell you—this would explain a lot."

Parker would be willing to bet it was the first time Tristan had ever laughed out loud while in bed with a woman, and the levity was still in his voice as he stroked his fingers down Carli's cheek, "Well, thank you, *mon cher*. It was pretty spectacular for me as well, and as soon as Master Parker's eyes roll back forward I'll bet he'll tell you the same."

"God in heaven, I'll need a little recovery time after that." *Like maybe a couple of days.* Christ, she'd stolen his mind with nothing more than a blowjob—what would happen when he was actually able to slide inside her? "Princess, you have a devil-blessed mouth, and I have every intention of showing you what I can do with my own, but right now we all need to get some rest." Just as he spoke the words, she tried valiantly to stifle a yawn. With a quick tug of the remaining silk tail, Carli's bound wrists sagged against the pillow free of their place at the headboard. Parker had to admit, the West brothers had done them a great favor when they'd put them in touch with a master metal magician in his home state of Texas—Clint was a wizard when it came to making their kinky decorating ideas a reality.

Tristan still lay on his side facing Carli, looking every bit as shell shocked as he felt himself. "I agree with Parker, *mon cher*, we all need sleep, but we're going to show you a bit more about the lifestyle first." Parker wanted to smile because he knew her thoughts weren't headed in the same direction as Tristan's.

One of the elements of the lifestyle The Knight's Club emphasized in each and every training session was the importance of aftercare that was, in a large part, due to the Master in Residence. Master Tristan Harris considered it an essential part of the scene and he made sure the other Masters at the club were as committed as he was. He swore subs needed that connection as much as the sexual release, there had been times Parker wondered if he wasn't trying to nurture the submissive they'd played with, hoping she'd magically morph into the woman they would want to share their lives with.

Cuddling finally gave way to cleaning up and by the time both men returned to bed, Carli lay curled like a contented kitten in the middle of Tristan's gigantic bed. And just as they had the last time she'd slept here, the two of them watched her for several minutes—but this time they did what he was finally willing to admit he'd wanted to do the last time, they slid into the bed with her. Parker smiled when she grumbled at being disturbed and cuddled into his side. God, she was just a little bit of a girl as his mama would say. Until tonight, their size had never been an issue when playing with a submissive, but Carli Walker wasn't a trained sub, nor was she a member of The Knight's Club—something they needed to address quickly.

When Parker woke up hours later, he couldn't hold back his chuckle at Carli's sleeping position—she'd turned ninety degrees so she was now laying with the side of her face pressed against his lower abdomen and her legs draped over Tristan in a pose worthy of Venus. The soft tumble of her hair fell in silky waves over his thighs and even in the dim light he could see the different colors glistening as they intertwined giving her hair the depth that, along with her nearly perfect facial features, had made her one of the most recognized faces in the world.

Hearing his phone vibrate on the bedside table for the third time in five minutes, Parker cursed under his breath. Sliding out from under her warmth, Parker immediately missed the connection and obviously Carli had noticed as well because despite the fact he'd moved his own pillow into his place, she hadn't been fooled by its warmth. "Where are you going? Is something wrong? What time is it? Is it Cressi?"

"Shhh, princess, go back to sleep for a bit. Don't worry about the time, you said last night you didn't have any appointments today, so I want you to catch up on some rest." He'd kept his voice quiet hoping she wouldn't completely surface from her drowsy state but she'd seemed to be rousing when Tristan pulled her around and tucked her against his chest.

"*Mon cher*, I want to hold you while we both sleep. Now, be a good girl and settle down again because I'm not ready to face the world just yet. Let's let Parker deal with the squires for a little longer." Parker didn't miss the reference to the personal servants who assisted the knights of the realm, but he wasn't sure Carli had. *You can take the boy out of the kingdom, but you'll never purge the kingdom from his blood.*

Chapter Eight

TRISTAN LEANED BACK in one of the boutique's comfortable wingback chairs holding his phone to his ear, listening as his parents peppered him with questions about Carli. It had only been a few days since he and Parker had moved Carli into the top floor of The Knight's Club and Tristan was already anxious to begin the renovations they'd planned to combine the two separate living spaces. There wasn't much to do, they'd been planning for this day when they originally set up both apartments, and while he didn't want to raise a family inside a kink club, he also knew that was a few years down the road. Tristan had decided to take Carli out for a bit of retail therapy because she'd been close to the breaking point. Between smothering her younger sister during her recovery and ironing out the final details for her upcoming photo shoots, the woman had been strung entirely too tight.

Parker had suggested they just take her down to the club and paddle her until she was floating happily in subspace, but since she wasn't technically a member yet that hadn't really been an option. They'd opted to handle Carli's membership application just as they did everyone else's, but were routing the paperwork through their respective seconds in command to avoid any appearance of impropriety on their parts. Integrity was more than a principal they paid lip service to—it really was the way they dealt with each and every situation. Ensuring their membership didn't feel as if they'd circumvented the rules for the woman in their bed, would be directly proportionate to how readily she would be accepted by both members and staff in the future.

Tristan watched Parker swat Carli sending her scurrying back into the dressing room, when he raised a brow in question, his friend simply grinned. Tristan wasn't sure why Parker was pushing her a bit again—but it appeared to be quickly becoming Parker's second favorite activity with their pretty sub. Twice during his conversation, his phone had vibrated with an incoming call and he'd finally given up and glanced at the screen, then he moved the phone to frown at the unknown number that reflected back at him. Refocusing his attention on his conversation, he laughed, "Mum, please don't go batty trying to get ready for our visit, and don't plan a lot for us to do because there are some security concerns right now with Carli." He made a mental note to speak with his dad about taking his mother into London for the first few days of their visit.

"Be sure you let James know what adjustments need to be made in the estate's security. We can also add staff if that would help." Tristan wasn't surprised his father had so quickly picked up on his concern, and updating the head of their family's security detail was definitely on his "To Do" list.

James Mikels was former SAS and one of the best security strategists in the world. The only thing that kept Parker from trying to recruit James was the fact he'd have to answer to Mary Elizabeth Harris, and his mother might look every inch the cultured aristocrat in public—usually, but everyone who knew her had nothing but respect for her ability to take someone apart if they had it coming. James had joined the Harris staff just over a year ago, coming on after the estate's enormous main house had been broken in to for the third time in a month. As a former Special Air Services member, he was a straight-up badass, to use the phrase his American friends were so fond of. The British Special Forces teams of the SAS were known as the world's best, it was the model used for every other Special Forces organization in the world. Tristan had done a broad spectrum of hand-to-hand combat training with masters in their respective disciplines, but James was one of the few sparring partners who managed to challenge him each and every time they'd faced off.

"I'll be sure to contact James, but I'm guessing Parker has already done so. Mum, we'll be staying in my suite so you needn't ready any of the other rooms in that wing of the house. But I would appreciate it if you would stock the small kitchen with fruit, wine, and cheese—oh, and Parker's beer." Tristan's phone beeped with an incoming message, but before he could check it he was interrupted by the sound of shouting coming from the dressing room area, "I have to go—I'll check in again before we head your way."

Disconnecting the call, he followed Parker pushing past a boutique employee who stood at the door to the dressing area, "You can't come in here. This area is for the ladies, men are not allowed past this point."

"Ma'am, you need to move—*now.*" Predictably, she responded as most people would to Parker's size and no nonsense tone of voice and quickly stepped to the side. "Carli?" Tristan heard the concern in Parker's voice and the fact he'd used her given name was also telling.

"*Mon cher,* where are you?" Just as he asked the question a young woman who at first glance reminded him of Carli stepped from behind one of the curtains giving them a snide smile before turning back to whisper something to whoever was behind her. Tristan would have bet his inheritance the woman was speaking to Carli, but without knowing for sure, he wasn't willing to pull the curtain aside. *"Mon cher.* Right fucking now." The bark of his tone made the young woman in front of them turn sharply in his direction leveling a glare Tristan knew she assumed would silence him.

"I'm here. It's alright, Mallory was just leaving. She's made her point." Carli's soft voice sounded from behind the woman standing before him. Tristan simply pushed her aside, letting Parker deal with her was a far better option at this point. Mallory—whoever she was, had just made an enormous mistake, she made two enemies she didn't need. He nor Parker would be particularly forgiving when it came to someone hurting Carli.

Stepping into the small dressing room, Tristan was surprised to see the woman sitting on the small bench against the mirror looking far different from the one he'd seen bantering with Parker just a few minutes earlier. Carli looked tired and defeated. The stark change in her demeanor made his blood boil. That look should never be in any woman's eyes and it bloody well wasn't ever supposed to be in *their* woman's eyes. *What the hell did that twit say to her anyway?* Carli wasn't crying—that he would have known how to handle, after all he dealt with sobbing women regularly at the club. However, the look of resigned exhaustion was what stopped him in his tracks. His heart felt as if someone was squeezing it in two and for the first time Tristan understood at least part of what his dad had been trying to explain to him—this was what love felt like.

Tristan knelt in front of her and pulled her trembling hands into his, "Talk to me, baby." His heart nearly broke as he watched her shoulders sag and he wondered for several seconds if she was going to answer. Tristan could hear the deep rumbling of Parker's voice interacting with someone whose voice was so shrill it reminded him of fingernails being pulled down a chalkboard—good God, just the thought made him want to shudder.

Carli's eyes were so green they made him think of the shamrocks of the Emerald Isle. They were shiny with unshed tears that she blinked quickly to clear. For the first time, she willingly sought his comfort, leaning forward laying her cheek against his shoulder. He didn't want to push her, but they really did need to know what the woman had said before Parker was forced to let her walk away. "Carli, is that someone you know?"

His question had evidently been enough to pull her out of the silent solace she'd found in his embrace, leaning back he saw her smile ruefully, "Yes, she's a photographer's assistant on my shoot crew, Mallory Brighten—she's also an aspiring model. Unfortunately, she is letting jealousy rule her choices instead of putting forth the effort to work for what she wants. She feels she is entitled to my help, simply because people have mentioned that she resembles me and we work together." He understood how someone who wasn't paying close attention might make that observation, but there were simply too many differences between the two women for professional modeling agents to make the mistake.

Carli had obviously read his expression correctly because this time her smile was genuine, "I know, I don't really see it either. She is very pretty, but she is far more slender and her hair colorist hasn't managed to duplicate what Mother Nature and my real mom gave me. But she really is beautiful and her career is only limited by her pettiness and dour attitude." When she paused, he tunneled his fingers under her hair until his palm was wrapped around the base of her skull. He didn't speak, he just waited for her to gather her thoughts and continue. Since they would be able to contact the woman again, there was no longer the same urgency to finding out what the woman had said, he wanted to let Carli process everything as much as possible.

"I don't know how she knew I was here. I don't believe her story that she just happened to be here shopping for our upcoming trip. I know it makes me sound catty, but she doesn't make enough money to shop here. Honestly, I probably wouldn't shop here either, holy shit have you looked at the prices on these clothes? It's insane what a little piece of flipping lace costs. I have no idea why Cressi even bothers buying beautiful panties when she said her men simply shred them."

Because Doms love the sound lace makes as it is ripped from their subs body. Anything that stands between me and your lovely pussy is going to be in tatters too, lovely girl.

Tristan didn't remember ever being relieved to hear a submissive curse, but he was nearly ecstatic about it now. Knowing she had recovered enough to swear made those words about the sweetest he'd ever heard. "That's another five, *mon cher*." When she shrugged and grinned, he shook his head, "I do believe you're testing me, baby. Not the best idea you've ever had, love. But since our afternoon has not turned out as Master Parker or I envisioned it would, perhaps we can tweak things a bit—rest assured, we will always meet any challenge you throw down…*always*."

Her breath stuttered as her eyes dilated until there was only a thin ring of brilliant green circling her pupils. Tristan heard Parker's low chuckle from the doorway, "I'm not sure, but I think our princess is more than a little turned on by your comment. And ordinarily I'd take great pleasure in testing my theory, but I'm anxious to get out of here. I don't know what that woman's problem is, but I'll know everything there is to know about her before tomorrow morning. I don't know about you two, but I'm finished shopping. The sales clerk is taking care of our purchases now and, princess, I've added a few things to what the two of you had agreed on. I don't want any arguments from you about my additions, either. Trust me, everything I've picked out is for Tristan's and my pleasure."

Tristan watched her stiffen and press her lips tightly together in an effort to not speak, *"Mon cher,* we are fully aware of the fact you do not *need* for us to buy your clothing. But, we enjoy spoiling you and if buying you clothes makes us happy, why would you want to argue?" Typically Tristan didn't like playing mind games with submissives—it had always seemed too close to manipulating the boundary of consensual power exchange. But Carli was going to require him to expand his repertoire a bit because her mind processed information at a blindly fast rate. Staying a step ahead of her would require a new mindset and he planned to do whatever it took to keep her.

"CRESSIDA, SIT DOWN. Your incessant pacing is not going to get the paperwork here any faster." She ignored Brodie's command and turned when her hand touched the wall in front of her. Her vision had been slowly improving, but when she was stressed things tended to become more blurred. She knew she should be resting, but her restless energy wouldn't let her settle down.

"I can't sit down, I'll explode if I do." Her vision was getting dimmer now and she knew it was because she was becoming upset. The doctors had mentioned that any elevation in her blood pressure would probably cause more swelling against her optic nerve, so everyone around her had been walking on eggshells. *And like that isn't tantamount to telling someone who is already angry to calm down. Nothing upsets me more than being told I shouldn't be upset. And do you think my husbands are going to do anything about it? Oh hell, no. I couldn't get a spanking out of this deal if my life depended on it.*

On her next pass by him, Brodie grabbed her arm pulling her close enough that she could see him despite her dimming vision. The stinging swat he gave her sent warmth skittering over her ass cheek and Cressi fought back the moan threatening to bubble up from her core. *More, please, more.* "We're keeping track, pet. And you are running up quite a tab. Do you know that Lawton has actually written a program to determine how long it will be until you can sit down again once you've been cleared by the doctors? I think he was tired of doing the math longhand. And just an FYI, Dr. Berstein is a Knight's Club member who knows exactly what we have in mind, so don't expect him to save your sweet little ass from everything you've got coming." Well, at least that explained why she'd thought his tone of voice seemed so familiar that first night.

Cressi would hear the amusement in his voice even if she couldn't see it in his expression. "That's just lame, really, I would have expected something much more creative from the two of you than some wimpy spreadsheet. You know what I think? I think you're losing your edge. I got hurt and now it's all sunshine and lollipops, it positively sickeningly sweet. And I swear if you turn vanilla on me I'm throwing myself off a bridge."

She hadn't meant to blurt out so much of what she was feeling, but somehow the words had circumvented her verbal filter and tumbled free before she'd had a chance to rein them in. She felt Brodie go completely still, the sort of stillness she'd come to associate with a Dom pushed too far. A part of her wanted to rejoice because maybe this was going to get her the kinky sex she'd been craving since she'd been hurt, but a part of her knew pushing her Doms rarely worked out well for her and the two of them were insanely creative when it came to punishing her.

"Where in God's creation did you get the impression we had gone soft on you, pet? I assure you that is *not* the case—do not mistake love and care with weakness. You have challenged every single person who has walked through that door the past few days, except our parents. And while Lawton and I are both amused by their exemption from your snarky attitude, it isn't going to be enough to save your lovely ass from all the punishments you've earned. Rest assured we will hold you accountable for each and every infraction, and we're more anxious than you know to do so."

The kiss he gave her was scorching and nothing like the chaste pecks she'd been getting for the past couple days. Cressi felt her knees start to weaken just before Brodie broke the kiss, she pressed closer wanting desperately to experience the intimacy they'd enjoyed before some crazed lunatic decided to send her ass over teakettle down a marble staircase. "Not here. Not now. You'll get what you need, pet—but not until Bernie assures us that it's safe. We won't ever take risks with your health, no matter how badly we want to fuck you senseless."

"I'm here to second that—and to let you know we're ready to go." Cressi jumped at the sound of Lawton's voice so close behind her, it was a testament to how distracted she'd been by Brodie's kiss that she hadn't heard him enter the room. "And, baby, the sooner you're healed, the sooner we can start getting you caught up on swats—because at this point, we'll be working on the list for months. You've been naughty and we've got some great plans for bringing you back in line."

Cressi's body was alight with desire, but at this moment it was centered on getting the hell out the damned hospital. The first thing she planned to do was take a nice long bath and soak the antiseptic smell off her skin. After that, all bets were off. She had every intention of circumventing whatever restrictions the doctors had given her. For the first time in days, Cressi felt more like her old self—and it felt damned good.

Chapter Nine

DALE ROBERTS STARED at the screen, the urge to kill the bitch suspected of pushing Cressida down the stairs coursing through his blood. She'd nearly killed his woman and ordinarily Carli Walker's safety was of no interest to him, but the assailant who'd hurt Cressida in an attempt to get to Carli had changed the game. Parker Daniels' team had finally named a suspect and that was good enough for Dale, he'd be tracking the investigation closely and if she was indeed guilty, law enforcement wouldn't stand a chance of getting to her first.

It made sense to him that she'd surfaced as a suspect, it was apparently common knowledge among Carli's crew that the woman felt Carli Walker was the only thing standing between her and superstardom. Mallory Brighten's computer had been embarrassingly easy to hack and her social media was littered with thinly veiled references to Ms. Walker. But the most damning evidence was the images she'd tried to delete—silly girl, once you use an image it is easy to trace back to you. She'd defaced pictures of Carli and posted them as a game for her followers. Evidently Ms. Brighten was also romantically involved with Phillip Gaines' latest boy-toy as well. Dale simply restored the pictures and then backed out of Mallory's computer so efficiently no one would ever know he'd been there, but he had made certain no one would miss the images he found buried there. He wouldn't plant evidence, because he was genuinely interested in finding the real culprit, but he had no intention of helping her hide her obsession with Carli Walker or her connection to Phillip Gaines' lover either.

Leaning back, he looked out over the surf pounding against the beach in a relentless rhythm as old as time and wondered what Cressida would think of his newest acquisition. The man who'd signed his seaside villa over in lieu of paying his debt had not been happy losing this small slice of heaven. But the place had everything Dale needed to keep Cressida safe from the men he knew would come looking for her—you had to say one thing about sex-slave traders, they certainly seem to have a knack for building a fortress to hide their merchandise. He wouldn't be able to get to her right away, but eventually they wouldn't be watching—and she'd be his.

CARLI FELT TRISTAN'S hand pressed firmly against the hollow at the base of her spine—that ultra-sensitive spot just above her ass where the heat of his hand was easily penetrating her clothing. The possessive touch warmed her entire body as they entered the private elevator that would whisk them upstairs, and although she'd previously considered that particular touch too forward on dates with other men, it now felt grounding. Tristan moved her to the back of the elevator, leaving room for Parker to follow them in, and push an elaborate series of numbers into the keypad.

"I'd never be able to remember that—I might have

been a business major, but memorizing strings of numbers is almost impossible for me. What time is it? I need to call Cressi and I should check in with Phillip, too. I'm hungry. Are you hungry?" Parker looked at her with his brow raised high, a move she'd come to realize meant he was somewhere between baffled and bemused, and she was betting it was a fifty-fifty shot for either of those right now. Carli knew she babbled when she was nervous. She was usually able to rein it in, but the small space coupled with the fact her body had been on a slow simmer since Tristan had promised to punish her was enough to scatter what little focus she was usually was able to pull together when she was near the two of them.

Her reputation as one of the most professionally focused and business savvy models in the industry was going to tank if any of her crew saw her with Parker and Tristan—damn these two men made her brain misfire. Yeah, one look at her starry-eyed, drooling self and her gossipy coworkers would set Twitter and Facebook on fire. Carli finally realized she'd been staring at Parker without really *seeing him*...and that his lips were moving. *Uh oh.*

"I swear to God she is looking right at me and not hearing me, and I have no idea how that is even possible."

"I'm not sure I've ever met a submissive who needs this lifestyle more than ours." Feeling Tristan lean over her shoulder to speak against the sweet spot just below her ear made Carli sway on her feet. "You need to stay in the moment, *mon cher*, letting your mind wander when you are with your Doms is a dangerous practice. Now, do as you've been told before you add to your punishment."

"I don't know what you said, I don't know how to explain the way my brain seems to leave my body when I'm with you two—it's embarrassing. I swear to all that's holy my IQ drops ten points when we're alone, you both probably think I'm some sort of dip-shit that can't tell her ass from a posy of petunias."

She heard Tristan growl behind her as Parker shook his head as if he really couldn't believe she'd managed to fuck up again. "Princess, I was trying to take your shovel away from you so you wouldn't continue to dig yourself deeper, but I'll be damned if you don't have a death grip on it." Carli blinked up at him wondering what in the hell he was talking about, when he grinned, "Strip, princess."

Blinking up at him in disbelief, she cocked her head to the side, "What? Here? Seriously? Why?"

"Let's see, that's two for not calling me Master either time you've spoken, five for the swearing, and another two for each of those questions. Another fifteen onto what you'd already accumulated today, keep it up and you'll still be too sore to sit down on the plane." All she could do was gape at him. The doors of the elevator slid silently open but no one moved. Deciding to cut her losses, she reached for the hem of her dress and slowly pulled it over her head.

Carli wasn't a fool, she knew exactly how her body looked, and after all, she was paid a lot of money to keep herself toned and moisturized to the point she swore she almost squished when she walked. And God knew she'd looked at enough tack sheets over the years to know each and every flaw. But seeing Parker's eyes darken with desire and his nostrils flare made her grateful for each and every minute of her beauty routine, she was even thankful for the time she spent being torture by her personal trainer even though she was convinced he was the devil in human form.

"All of it, princess." For several seconds Carli stood completely still trying to process Parker's words, and then she remembered she was still wearing the demi bra and thong she'd donned for their shopping trip. Removing both pieces, she handed them to Tristan since he'd been the one to take the dress from her hands earlier. "You're beautiful, but what you don't realize is that your real beauty comes from the inside. You are under the mistaken impression Master Tristan and I are seeing the outside—like everyone else. And while I'll admit, the outside is stunning, it's the core that interests us. The woman who mothered her younger sister when her own mother was taken too soon. The woman who changed the direction of her own life—putting her dreams on hold to take a high paying modeling position so she could pay for her sister's education. The woman who has managed to parlay her earnings into an impressive personal fortune by making incredibly wise financial investments. The woman who wasn't afraid to meet the challenge thrown down by a couple of sexual Dominants and is discovering something new about herself every day. *That* is the woman who interests us, because she is brilliant, loyal, and fearless."

Carli was completely stunned. Nothing that had happened today could have prepared her for Parker's words. She wasn't sure she'd ever felt as *exposed* as she did in that moment and she suddenly understood that he'd had her strip intentionally to enhance the feeling. He'd wanted her to understand everything about her was open to their perusal. "I see understanding dawning in your expression, princess. Yes, we want you to understand you have no need to hide anything about yourself from us—in fact, we'll work very hard to insure you don't until you reach the point your soul understands it isn't necessary."

Tristan moved around to stand in front of her, his perceptive expression taking in everything, "The part of the lifestyle that first appealed to me was the intimacy involved. Not only the physical connection, which is earth moving when it's *right*, but also the depth of the emotional connection I saw in couples who understood baring their souls to one another was the way to forge lifelong bonds stronger than anything the world could throw at them. I believe the three of us can form a bond every bit as strong as those I have admired, but it won't always be easy and it will require trust on a level you will probably struggle with for a while."

Oh she didn't have any trouble imaging that they would push her, God, they'd been pushing since the beginning. What she was unsure of was her ability to meet the challenge. She didn't really have any experience with long-term commitments; she hadn't gone on more than three dates with one man since college. However, wasn't that the point, her life was full to the brim, but was there any real substance that would see her through life's highs and lows? Would the people who seemed to take up so much of her time *be there for her* if she wasn't Carli Walker, model extraordinaire? And did she have anything to lose by trying?

Nodding her understanding, Parker and Tristan both shook their heads, "Not good enough, princess. We need to hear the words." Nodding to the open door, he asked, "Are you ready to step over the threshold and surrender yourself into our care tonight? You always have your safe words—don't ever forget that. But save those, you are ours."

Tristan's eyes had darkened until they reminded her of the color of a moonlit sky at midnight...the blue was the so deep you'd mistake it for black if you weren't looking closely. "Ask your questions now, *mon cher*, because once you step to the other side you'll only speak when asked a direct question until we've finished tonight. While we aren't twenty-four/seven Doms, we are always Doms."

"I don't know exactly what that means, Master Tristan. And, I know we have dabbled for the past couple of days, but this feels like something entirely different." Carli knew they'd hear the trepidation in her voice, and she knew she'd been right when his expression softened for just a second.

"It is different. And what I meant was, while we won't require high protocol all the time, we will expect you to at least listen to our advice and counsel. We won't lay down the law, as you Americans are so fond of saying, unless it's a question of your personal safety—in those instances what we tell you will be non-negotiable." Most of what they'd just outlined Carli had heard from Cressida—obviously the four men had similar views related to the lifestyle, though Carli guessed the two standing in front of her were more hard line in their views.

"Remember, princess, safe words are not to be used if you simply want to change the direction things are moving. If we think you've used it to manipulate the situation, we'll end the scene and not begin again. This is about trust, you either trust us or you don't. Questions are understandable, you are, after all, new to the lifestyle and we'll make allowances for that. But you'll get far more from the experience if you let go and simply put yourself in our hands."

"*Mon cher*, we aren't expecting perfection, just compliance and trust." They made it sound so easy, and even as inexperienced as she was, Carli knew full well it was going to be very difficult to give up control.

Her entire world centered on her ability to control her life. But, when she'd asked her sister how on earth she managed to let Lawton and Brodie control so much of her life, Cressi had shaken her head and laughed. "I haven't given up control, Carli. It's a power exchange, and believe me I'm getting the better deal...by a long shot. I don't have to worry about what I *should be doing*...does he want me to put my hands in his hair, caress him in a certain way—none of those things enter my mind because I know they will tell me exactly what I'm supposed to do. It's liberating, all I have to do is what they ask me to do and enjoy. And I assure you the paybacks are a thousand times better than anything you've ever experienced. Seriously, you haven't lived until you've experienced the kind of pleasure that makes you feel as though the top of your head is about to blow off."

Carli hadn't been entirely convinced, but she wasn't going to argue about something she really didn't fully understand—and quite frankly, the idea of experiencing the kind of pleasure her sister was talking about sounded more than just a little bit appealing. *Compliance and trust*...that's all Tristan said they required—could she do those two things? Yes—probably...well, she could sure try. And if she found a few dozen killer orgasms along the way, all the better.

Decision made, Carli took a deep breath and stepped off the elevator.

PARKER FELT THE breath he'd been holding rush from between his lips when Carli squared her shoulders and stepped from the elevator, but he didn't let his relief show as he and Tristan made quick work of moving her down the hallway. When Carli started to turn toward the bedroom, it was Tristan who corrected her, "Not this time, *mon cher*. We have something entirely different in mind." Stopping in front of the door leading to what subs had lovingly nicknamed *The Treehouse* because of its unique location overlooking the building's large atrium and the fact it had been designed to look like an old English forest. They'd decided to make their playroom entirely unexpected. There were plenty of castle and dungeon themed rooms available to them downstairs, so they'd opted to turn their private play area into a place much more interesting.

The decorator they'd hired was also a club member and former set director for several well-known Broadway productions, so he'd brought a unique skill set to the project. Watching him design and create specialized equipment that looked like standing and fallen trees, and then incorporate a stone cliff facade into the back wall had been fascinating. The entire area was essentially a mezzanine, open to the areas of the club below until the hidden glass partitions were activated and slid silently into place. Tristan's favorite piece of equipment was the fallen tree spanking bench, but Parker's was the swing.

Hanging from an open rafter disguised to look like a giant tree branch, the swing was comprised of four smooth pieces of birch in an adjustable rectangle. The submissive straddled the swing leaving her pussy and anus completely exposed—and available. The detachable backrest was great for tilting a sweet, cooperative sub to the best angle, but when that support piece was left off—a sub's core muscles got a great workout as well. The designer's use of ropes camouflaged as vines and synthetic bark that didn't chafe the skin made the space not only gorgeous but safe for the women they'd played with in the past. Every submissive in

The Knight's Club had heard about the playroom assuring they'd always had plenty of play partners.

For some reason, thinking about the other women who had passed through the door of their playroom sent a pang of regret through Parker and the feeling shocked him. He'd never felt guilty about his sexual history and it surprised him that he did now. Shaking it off, he refocused his attention on the woman standing between them and wanted to smile at the look of astonishment on her sweet face. Her eyes were wide with childlike wonder as she took in her surroundings and he knew she'd completely forgotten about her promise to surrender herself to them for the evening.

"*Mon cher*, welcome to our playroom. Since this is your first visit here, we're going to show you around first—but in the future, you'll be expected to observe a very strict set of rules whenever you enter this space, do you understand?" Parker watched as Carli blinked several times as if that would help her process Tristan's words. He knew from experience that particular look meant they'd be reiterating whatever piece of information they'd given her again, when they actually had her full attention.

"Yes, I understand, though I'll want you to explain exactly what you expect." When Tristan nodded, she returned her attention to the room, "It's just simply breathtaking, I'm not sure I've ever seen anything like it outside of a commercial setting. Who designed it? It's stunning and even I can see there are secrets hidden here—secrets I'm certain are all about sexual pleasure." For just a second Parker watched as her enthusiasm dimmed and he would have bet his entire share of Daniels' Oil he knew what had gone through her mind, and he watched as the shield he'd seen in her eyes so often slid quickly into place.

Gone was the look of child-like enthusiasm and in its place was the cool indifference of professional appreciation, and Parker could almost feel her pulling back.

Stepping in front of her, Parker made certain he was close enough she was forced to tilt her head back to meet his gaze, "Don't. You're overthinking this and that is simply not going to work. Yes, we've played with other submissives here before, but I can honestly tell you I've never enjoyed watching anyone's reaction as much as I enjoyed yours. But now, seeing that wall of ice move into place isn't working for me—not even a little, princess."

"*Mon cher*, we can't change our past, and honestly I'm not sure I would even if I could, because everything we've done up to this point has made us better Doms. It also means we recognize a once in a lifetime opportunity when we see it and, *mon amōre,* you are exactly that."

Chapter Ten

CRESSIDA WAS DISCOURAGED by the bone-deep exhaustion swamping her as the three of them moved into the private elevator that would take them to the top of the Templar Enterprises Group building. She'd almost fallen asleep on the short ride from the hospital, and the only thing keeping her awake now was her frustration at not being able to see clearly—damn, if she ever got her hands on the maniac who pushed her down the hotel's marble staircase she wasn't going to be responsible for her actions. Cressi still couldn't believe with all the electronic surveillance in the hotel her assailant had essentially disappeared without a trace.

"Pet?" She could hear the concern in Brodie's voice, but it also sounded far away—and since when did this elevator rotate? She felt herself falling but strong arms caught her before she hit floor, even through the fog Cressi recognized Brodie's touch as he lifted her into his arms, "I am adding this to your punishment, pet. When are you going to learn it's not only okay to ask for help, it's *expected*? You are compromising your safety and I think we've made it crystal clear that isn't acceptable."

"Baby, your tab just passed Thanksgiving, I'm suggesting you rein it in a bit since I'd like to see you sit through some of the great Christmas shows on Broadway I'm sure my mom is planning to drag you to." Cressi wanted to snicker at his words, but it turned into racking sobs before she knew what was happening. "Hey, what's this? You don't have to go if you don't want to, damn, baby, don't cry." Cressi wasn't sure what was happening, but she knew it had nothing to do with what Lawton had said, she loved his mom and was looking forward to anything they could do together.

"Law, I think this is one of those mood swings they warned us about. Remember, the second neurologist mentioned erratic emotional responses to everyday situations was a common side effect of closed head trauma." *What? Nobody mentioned that to me.* "The bad news is our wife is crying and I fucking hate it. But, the good news is they identified this as the next stage of her healing process so this means she's getting better."

Cressi couldn't hold back the giggle that bubbled up in the middle of her sobs when she thought about the absurdity of what was happening around her. *Seriously, it sounds like one of those late night episodes of Abbott and Costello. I feel like I'm living an old variety show watching the 'Who's on first' skit.* "I'm sorry, I really don't know what's come over me. It's like I don't have any control over my emotions, and it's been like this for days—damn it to doorknobs, I'm even driving myself crazy. I don't mean to be a pain in the ass, really—I just can't seem to help it. I open my mouth and *crazy* comes out—it sounds like my voice, but not like something I would say to anyone…well, except my sister. Crispy critters, I'm worried my head will spin around on my shoulders like that girl who was possessed. And now you're keeping some sort of crazy punishment score, I'm in so much trouble and I don't even remember half of why. I don't like being in trouble." She was sobbing again, her tears soaking the shoulder of Brodie's formerly pristine dress shirt. He'd sat down on the settee in their bedroom and Lawton pulled her shoes off and began rubbing her feet with his strong hands. Both men knew how much she loved having the arches of her feet massaged and they'd quickly learned how to exploit the information. They'd used promises of massages to finagle a wide variety of special favors. Shifting on Brodie's lap, Cressi moaned in pleasure through her tears making both men chuckle.

"I'm not sure we'd taken into account your snarkiness might well be related to your injury, so we'll reconsider and negotiate the punishments, pet. But something you said needs to be addressed—don't ever confuse our desire to correct a behavior as disappointment in who you are as a person. We aren't trying to change what makes you unique—after all, that's the woman we fell in love with. We're simply trying to help you become all we know you can be."

"Think of us as coaches with benefits." God she loved them both so much, they could make her smile even when there didn't seem to be anything to smile about. Marrying them had been the answer to her prayers, and even now...when she couldn't see them clearly, she knew exactly what their expressions were. Lawton's smile would be slightly crooked, reminding her of an ornery boy who knew exactly how to annoy the girl sitting next to him in class. Brodie's expression would be one of cool assessment. He'd be watching her closely—cataloging her every reaction, storing the information for reference later. They understood her when she didn't understand herself, and their ability to see into her soul—breaking down complex emotional responses so she could see past her preconceived ideas had always been easy for them. The research she'd done before approaching Tristan to join the Knight's Club had referred to a good Dom's superior intuitive skills, but Cressi thought it was simply because they cared enough to watch, listen…and *hear* what the submissive in their care was saying.

"Baby, please stop crying—it isn't going to help the swelling at all and it's breaking my heart."

"Come on, let's get you into the shower. I know you said you were anxious to wash the hospital smell from your hair and skin, we'll all take a quick shower and then have a snack before resting. If I'm not mistaken, there is a large fruit and cheese plate already waiting for us. It seems the staff has taken a fancy to you, pet." Cressi smiled at the thought of the elderly couple who managed the building's custodial staff. Clifton and Anabelle Marin had been with T.E.G. from the beginning, Clifton managing the maintenance of the building while Anabelle managed a much smaller staff assigned to Lawton and Brodie's personal spaces. Since Cressi had already been friends with the couple, they'd been spoiling her by keeping all her favorite foods stocked in both kitchens since she'd moved in.

Before their shower was finished, Cressi turned to Brodie and pressed her cheek against his chest, "I'm so tired, I don't think I can do this without help."

His arms tightened around her and before she realized what was happening he'd picked her up into his arms. "Pet, you've pleased us both very much by asking for help."

It seemed to Cressi as if they'd just stepped into the shower, but when Lawton stepped up and finished rinsing the conditioner from her hair she realized she'd been standing just outside the warm spray of water staring off in an exhausted stupor. "Baby, it really isn't a sign of weakness to let us help you. We love you and helping you heal is an honor and privilege. Now, let's get a snack before you rest. You'll heal faster now that you're home. Hospitals are insane places and the only reason you got any rest at all is because Mom kept sending people down to guard the door."

Twenty minutes later, she'd eaten and finished the large glass of water they'd insisted she drink. With her eyelids drooping, Cressi was grateful for the chance to curl up in bed with her men. *I'm the luckiest woman in the whole world and I'm going to get better, I won't be a burden to any- one—I just won't.*

LAWTON STARED DOWN at his sleeping wife, overcome with emotion when he thought about the scars her childhood had left, and felt his blood begin to boil. "How could a father make his daughter feel so insecure? How could he not cherish her?"

"No fucking clue, but I assure you, I'm feeling the same anger you are. There isn't anything about her that's a burden, there is so much we could do to him but I'd much rather let karma take care of it. We need to focus our attention on her healing and finding out who's responsible for shoving her down the stairs."

"Parker feels as though they have a solid suspect and mentioned showing Cressida a few pictures to see if there was anything about the woman that seems familiar once her vision clears. But personally I think it's going to be the voice that triggers recognition." Lawton wanted to get a video of the woman, but wasn't sure they would have time since she was supposed to be accompanying Carli on her shoot—if their new sister-in-law could be persuaded to leave the country without assurance her little sister was going to fully recover.

When his phone vibrated on the bedside table, Lawton looked over and saw it was a call from Parker's younger sister, Olivia. Not wanting to disturb Cressida, he let the call go to voice mail. He'd missed a call from her earlier but she hadn't left a message, hopefully she'd let him know what she needed this time. It wasn't uncommon for her to call him from time to time with questions about programming he'd helped her create, but it was odd she hadn't left a message.

OLIVIA DANIELS DROPPED into an open seat on the commuter train and glared at her phone. Seriously? Didn't any of the Knights answer their damned phones anymore? She had called three of the four men and none had answered in the past twenty-four hours. *Glad I'm not dodging bullets—yet.* As an investigative researcher for the Nuclear Regulatory Commission, Olivia was one of several physicists who assessed various nuclear programs operating in and around the county—ensuring they were being operated safely. But six months ago she'd been recruited by the Central Intelligence Agency and from that point until now, her life had been slowly unwinding. Well, slowly until two days ago...and then everything had spiraled out of control so fast she was still trying to figure out how she'd ended up boarding a train at midnight in Washington DC with nothing but a small rolling case and her backpack in hopes she would make it to the small airport in New Jersey and somehow get on board the Templar Enterprises Group's jet before it left for London.

Thank God she'd called her mom early to wish her a happy birthday, if she had waited until tomorrow morning, Liv would have missed her best chance of getting out of the country. She needed help and she knew it, but until her brother or one of his business partners answered her call, she was on her own. Liv hadn't wanted to alert her mom that she was in trouble, so she'd asked about her brother just as she always did, without mentioning how desperate she was to make contact with him. Older than Liv by more than a decade, Parker had always been her champion and protector. Of course she'd rarely had a date with the same boy twice during high school because Parker had always mysteriously managed to be home the rare weekends a guy was brave enough to ask her out. She'd continually accused her mother of selling her out, but in hindsight—given her brother's penchant for all things electronic, he'd probably hacked her phone. *Too bad he isn't as interested in my calls now as he was my damned date to prom.*

Settling back into her seat, Olivia sent up a silent prayer that whoever had broken into her apartment hadn't still been watching when she'd returned home. She'd known immediately someone had been in her home even though they'd obviously been meticulous in the their efforts to hide the fact they'd searched what was supposed to be her sanctuary. What she didn't know was who or why. Parker and T.E.G. were her best hope at unraveling the mystery, but she knew her brother well enough to know he'd cancel whatever trip he was going on to stay stateside and help when what she really wanted was to get away from the threat so she could think clearly.

Ordinarily, Liv Daniels ran headfirst into challenges, always believing in the old adage about "running to the roar." But there was something very different about this…something about the whole situation felt much more malevolent. This was more than someone breaking in looking for her grandmother's diamond bracelet—which, along with all her other jewelry, had been left untouched. She didn't know what they wanted and honestly couldn't even fathom having anything someone thought was that important. During the short time she'd been in her apartment, she'd grabbed her passport and packed up all her files and electronics. A quick stop at her bank and she'd withdrawn enough cash to fund a small nation, because she wasn't going to let anyone track her movements by using credit cards, damn it, she thought they should at least have to do the leg-work if they wanted to know where she was.

If her calculations were right and her brother wasn't running ahead of schedule like he so often did, she might make it in time to talk her way onto the jet. If Lawton was flying, she was confident she'd be able to talk her way aboard and hopefully he'd be able to dissuade Parker from throwing her out over the ocean once he found out she was onboard. He was going to hit the ceiling when he found out what a mess she'd landed in—she hadn't told her family about her recruitment into the world of espionage for a reason. Knowing she'd be facing off with the most vocal of those reasons all too soon, Liv leaned back against the cracked leather seat and closed her eyes. She tried to calm the chaotic sea of emotions and shattered thoughts cluttering her mind and hoped to get a few minutes respite and rest.

Chapter Eleven

TRISTAN WATCHED CARLI'S eyes soften to his admission that he considered the gift of her submission a once in a lifetime opportunity. If they could earn her trust, it would be their most valuable possession. Every time he touched her, his soul screamed *MINE!* She didn't know they were planning to leave for London tomorrow. Parker's staff had packed for her, but it hadn't been much of an issue since they'd taken her shopping today.

Tristan had asked his dad to take his mom into London for a few days, giving the three of them some time alone at the estate. Even though Tristan still had his own wing of the main house, he was certain Carli would appreciate a couple of days to adjust to her surroundings without his parents present. While he loved his mother dearly, he was well aware of how over-the-top and overwhelming she could be. Mary Elizabeth Harris was a carefree spirit with an effervescent personality, she'd won over the prim and proper members of his father's aristocratic family, including members of the royal family. Her enthusiasm often seemed a bit much at first, but her zeal for life was simply too contagious for most people to resist for very long.

Setting aside all thoughts of what tomorrow held, Tristan watched Carli walk slowly around their playroom. She'd asked Parker a few questions, but nothing either of them hadn't been asked before. It was clear she was still working to keep them at arm's length, her realization they'd had other women here had obviously been a larger issue than he'd anticipated it might be. He'd assumed she would be more sexually experienced than she was and he could only assume that was part of what was hanging her up. Hopefully she would quickly accept the truth that both he and Parker were ready to move on to their future—assuming Parker accepted the truth before his commitment phobia shone through too clearly.

He suspected Parker had already been falling for Carli before Tristan had even met her, but he doubted his friend was ready to admit it yet. It hadn't take Tristan any time at all to see all Parker and Carli's bickering was just a form of foreplay—an annoying form at times, but foreplay nonetheless. Watching the two of them now, they'd settled into a much less tenuous relationship. Parker was shadowing her as she moved around the space—standing nearby, but not hovering as she explored. Tristan listened in as Parker answered her questions, correcting inaccurate assumptions or information he was sure she'd probably gotten from the internet. It never ceased to amaze him how much bogus information was out there about various elements of sex play. And time and again he'd talked to prospective club members whose sole source of information about the lifestyle was some damned internet chat room, and he'd spent the majority of several initial interviews correcting inaccurate information.

"*Mon cher*, come to me." It was time to get started and he was suspicious she was running out of questions and he could almost feel her nervousness building. Time to show her that her imagination was her worst enemy in this circumstance. When she was standing in front of him, he smiled down at her as she shifted from foot to foot. "Don't get caught up in what you *think* is going to happen. We've reviewed safe words several times, but I want to plant that seed in your mind once again." While he'd been speaking, Tristan had been stroking the backs of two fingers over her nipple.

Over the years, he learned one of the perks of dealing with models was that they were usually far more at ease with their bodies and Carli was no exception. Rather than being uncomfortable being naked, Carli seemed to have completely forgotten she was totally exposed to their touch. Her nipples had drawn up into tight peaks reminding him of the sweet raspberries he used to nibble on while wandering around the estate where he'd grown up. *I'll bet her berries are just as sweet and sucking them is going to be one of my greatest pleasures.*

"You are beautiful, *mon cher,* and we are looking forward to spending a lot of time in this room exploring different aspects of the lifestyle with you. There are so many ways for us to give you pleasure—and we'll try as many of those when we're all three comfortable enough to push the boundaries, although I'll warn you we both have a couple of hard limits as well."

"I'm confident our hard limits aren't going to be an issue—and I'm sure they aren't going to come into play tonight, so let's get started. I believe you have earned several swats."

"Several indeed. Twenty at my count." Tristan watched her eyes widen in surprise. *Yes, mon amore, I kept track.*

"That's a lot of swats for an untrained submissive, princess. Hell, the way Tristan swings a paddle that's a lot for most subs." *Nice, Parker—absolutely brilliant, terrified is such a nice look for our woman. Not!* Tristan hoped like hell his friend had a plan for this conversation because it was headed in the wrong direction as far as he could see. "I have a suggestion—I think we should do some experimenting." Tristan had shared women with Parker since they were freshmen in college, so he knew him almost as well as he knew himself—but this was something entirely new. Parker Daniels was usually all about the rules and protocol, much like Tristan, so hearing him deviate from that was an interesting twist. Tristan was holding out hope that Parker was getting closer to admitting this woman was the one—and that she should belong to them forever.

"Well, do tell because I'm always interested in a good experiment. What did you have in mind for our naughty little submissive?" He'd been thrilled when Carli had sparked back to life cursing because it had been such a huge improvement over the disheartened expression he'd seen when he first stepped into the dressing room, and it had given them the perfect excuse to bring her into their playroom.

"I'll explain while we get her into position." Parker's words sent a shudder through her and Tristan wanted to smile at the sweet scent of her arousal as they secured her to the spanking bench.

Good to know our little sub's body is focused on arousal and not fear.

CARLI'S MIND STARTED to cloud as soon as she felt the first straps fasten her to what they'd called a spanking bench. The thing looked like a fallen log to her, but she'd quickly learned the heavy vines and large leaves were actually well camouflaged Velcro straps that ensured she wasn't able to move even a fraction of an inch. She'd been grateful her legs weren't as widespread as she'd seen some subs in the pictures online, but her gratitude didn't last long. Even through the fog clouding her mind, Carli heard a mechanical whirl a heartbeat before she felt herself being tilted forward and her legs moving apart. *So much for retaining even a thin thread of modesty—good God Gertie.*

While they'd fastened the straps Tristan and Parker had touched her continually—there hadn't been a moment that one of them didn't have a hand on her and that had gone a long way in grounding her. One of the things Carli hated the most about modeling was the necessity of having people she didn't feel any connection to touching her. They yanked clothes from her as soon as she was out of view of the public and then pulled the next garment on with little thought about respecting her personal space. The sharp sound of flesh colliding with flesh sounded a split second before her right ass cheek was seared with fire. "Fuck that hurt, give a girl a warning next time." The words escaped before Carli's brain had a chance to sensor them and she knew immediately she'd just added to her punishment. *Damn it, if I'd just been paying attention I would have been able to keep quiet...maybe.*

Parker squatted down in front of her, his grin was almost feral, "Princess, I'm not sure I've ever seen Master Tristan turn quite that shade of red before, I'm worried he's going to have a stroke so I suggest you choose your words much more carefully." Carli wanted to smack him— *really* wanted to smack him, it was probably a blessing her bound hands kept her from giving in to the temptation.

Before she realized what was happening five more swats landed in rapid succession and these were spread over her entire ass, making it feel as if someone had set her skin on fire. But she'd been prepared, so she'd been able to silence the string of curses that had blasted through her mind. "Take a breath, princess." Carli gasped, drawing in several deep breaths. "Open your eyes and look at me, Carli." *What?* She hadn't even realized she'd closed her eyes, and when she finally managed to follow Parker's command, she saw they were still face-to-face. She was surprised to feel the tears streaking down her cheeks. "I want you to think about your answer before you speak—now, tell me exactly what you're feeling."

Was he serious? Her ass felt like it was on fire…and, well…if she was honest, the heat seemed to have spread to her pussy as well. Her nipples were throbbing and wasn't that weird since no one had even touched them? Deciding honesty was her best option, Carli explained how her body was reacting, adding that she wasn't thrilled with the experience. "*Mon cher,* this isn't really for your pleasure. We are simply trying to remind you cursing is unacceptable. Now, you've told us how your mind is processing the experience, let's see how your body is responding."

Before she had a chance to ask what he meant, she felt his fingers sliding smoothly through the very wet folds of her pussy. "Oh God." He'd barely touched her and she could already feel her body racing toward release. Cressi had tried to explain the symbiotic relationship between pleasure and pain, insisting they were simply two sides of the same coin, but Carli hadn't been convinced—until now. She didn't know *why* it worked for her, as a matter of fact if she let herself think about it too much she knew she'd be embarrassed by her reaction, but another sharp slap on her ass startled her out of her thoughts.

"Stop thinking so much, *mon cher.* Your job is to *feel.*

Thinking is not required in the playroom. You have to do enough of that outside of this space. Let go of all those inner judgments and just listen to your body rather than your mind for a change." His fingers were working absolute magic and she wanted to come so badly, but something was blocking the track she'd been racing down and damned if she knew what it was. "You're thinking again and it's causing you an awful lot of trouble, sweet sub. When you truly let go, fully put yourself in our hands, your pleasure will come with just a single word from one of your Masters."

Parker's warm lips pressed a kiss against the tender spot below her ear before his teeth gently closed over her earlobe. She tried to push closer, but his growl stilled her movement, "Stay where we put you, princess. Goddammit to hell you are so responsive. I want to fuck you into oblivion. Master Tristan is going to insert the last plug and then switch to a flogger. The last of your punishment is going to feel entirely different because this portion is all about control."

They'd been using butt plugs on her for several days, gradually increasing the sizes and knowing this was the last one meant they planned to take her together soon. Just the thought of being between them—having them both buried deep in her body made her pussy convulse and she felt the moisture stream down the inside of her thighs. "Oh, *mon amour*, that's the prettiest thing I think I've ever seen. Your honey rushed out to greet me, you're anxious for us to fuck you at the same time, aren't you, sweet girl?"

"Oh, yes. I'm scared, but I still want it so badly I can barely think about anything else." Carli didn't care how desperate her voice sounded, she needed to come, and nothing else mattered in that moment. The plug was stretching her to the point the ring of muscle around her anus was burning, but when it finally slid into place she was panting with need. "Please, oh God, please help me come."

"All in good time, princess. And just for the record, you are not allowed to come until one of us gives you permission. Your pleasure belongs to us—therefore your orgasms belong to us. Perhaps I can help distract you." Carli was certain she knew what he had in mind, the man certainly seemed to love the way she sucked him all the way to the back of her throat. He was immediately pressing the tip of his cock against her lips, painting them with the pearly pre-cum that had beaded there. Snaking her tongue out, she moaned as his salty taste lit up her taste buds. "Jesus, Joseph, and Mary, princess, when you moan against the head it vibrates all the way to my root. Fuck, your mouth is lethal."

Carli felt the soft strands of the flogger caressing her skin, but focusing on Parker's pleasure was distracting her enough to stave off her own impending release—at least temporarily. Since neither of them had given her permission to come, Carli was grateful for the reprieve—short as it was. The falls of the flogger increased in intensity so subtly she'd barely noticed until she felt Parker withdraw a second after she'd felt his cock swell—a sure sign he was close to coming. Losing the contact made her growl in frustration. "Don't worry, princess, you'll get my cock again very soon."

At the same time, Carli heard the flogger clatter to the floor and the sound of Tristan's voice filled her ears just as his fingers filled her wet channel, "Come for us, *mon amore.*" Carli saw an explosion of light before she even realized she'd closed her eyes, as her entire body responded to the command. Waves of pleasure washed over her until she wondered if they'd ever end. When the pounding pleasure finally subsided she sagged, completely spent. "Oh, no, sweet sub, no rest for you."

"We have plans for you, princess." Carli didn't know what they had planned, but she sure hoped they wouldn't notice if she snoozed through it.

Chapter Twelve

TRISTAN HAD THE straps loosened and Carli cradled in his arms in seconds. He followed Parker, who'd gotten into position at the edge of the bed quickly. Tristan lifted Carli and helped settle her over Parker as his friend pushed his cock into her sweet pussy. "Holy hell, her vaginal muscles as still quivering, don't waste any time, between her sweet mouth and this—I'm not going to last long." Tristan had no intention of wasting any time, he needed to be inside her and that pretty little rosette had finally been prepared enough he knew she wasn't going to feel anything but the sweetest pain—the kind sure to drive her insane with pleasure.

Grabbing a small tube of lube, he slid his hand up and down the length of his cock enjoying the slippery feel of the lubricant he preferred as it spread smoothly over his veins and ridges. The earthy scent of sesame oil filled the air and he knew it wouldn't be long until the smell of the specially mixed oil alone would be enough to make Carli's pussy dampen in anticipation. Tristan removed the plug as Parker pulled Carli against his chest and Tristan could hear him whispering encouragement to her as he banded his arms tightly around her back. It was important that she was secured, preventing her from surging back before he'd properly stretched her rear opening—he and Parker had both seen subs who'd required emergency care because they'd shredded delicate tissues by pushing back prematurely against the intrusion. It was never pleasant and not something they wanted the woman in their care to experience.

"*Mon cher*, let your Master hold you—it is important that you stay still until I'm fully seated in your perfect little ass. As you know, we don't always give you *carte blanche* to speak during a scene, but you have it for this evening. We want you to tell us what is going through your mind, it's important that we know we're getting you where you need to be for this to be a pleasurable experience." The truth was he was worried she would hate it and he wasn't sure where that would leave them since having her between them would play such an integral part of the polyamorous relationship they had always dreamed of.

Massaging the fragrant oil into the tight ring of muscles eased them back open slowly, Tristan could feel them relaxing as he pressed first one finger and then two into the sweet hole. Withdrawing his fingers, he let a stream of oil trickle over the opening as he pressed his tip against the gateway to pleasure, applying a firm and constant pressure let the muscles flower open for him. By the time he'd finally worked himself past the outer of muscles, he could feel the sweat on his brow and Carli was panting beneath him. Parker's voice had a ring of desperation when he spoke from beneath the soft woman between them, "Don't stall, buddy, or you're going to be playing alone. She is about to launch into space."

"Oh dear God, please move, I can't take it. I'm so full I'm going to burst. Please do something." Oh, they fully intended to do something, and knowing she was enjoying the experience was all the motivation Tristan needed.

Within seconds he and Parker set up a slow rhythm, alternating their thrusts so one of them was always seated deep in their sweet woman, and Carli's response was explosive. Tristan felt his body responding to hers on such a deep level he wasn't sure it was even physical, he felt like their souls had been fused together the moment they all three reached climax, coming at exactly the same moment.

Shouts filled the air and it took every ounce of strength Tristan possessed to keep from collapsing on top of Carli. He kept his elbows locked as he sucked in huge gulps of air. Leaning down carefully, he pressed a kiss between Carli's shoulder blades, *"Mon amour,* you are exquisite—and all ours, don't ever forget that."

PARKER LEANED AGAINST the wall of the shower and shuddered beneath the spray of cold water. By the time they'd gotten their exhausted sub out of the shower, she'd been fast asleep. Christ, who knew a wet woman was so damned hard to hang onto when she was completely limp in your arms. Smiling to himself, Parker shut down the frigid water he'd hoped would deflate the hard-on he'd had since tucking a totally bare Carli between the sheets of Tristan's bed. *Since when doesn't an icy shower take the wind out of your sails?* Fuck it, talking to his cock showed just how fried his brain was—damn the woman had rocked him to the very depths of his soul. He'd already been struggling to deny the strength of their connection, but damn if she hadn't just blown that all to hell. Was he ready to settle down with one woman for the rest of his life? His head was still saying no, but the inner voice that had been so skeptical didn't sound nearly as committed to the negativity now that he knew what it felt like to have her between them.

Pulling on a pair of jersey pants, Parker made his way down to his office. He needed to make sure everything was in order for their trip. They hadn't mention leaving early to Carli simply because they preferred to avoid the argument that was certain to ensue, but there was no way he was allowing Carli to fly commercial considering the attack on her sister. And after her altercation with a coworker at the boutique he was even more convinced his decision to use the T.E.G. jet was a solid one.

Remembering the call he'd missed from Olivia, he dialed her number but the call went directly to voice mail. His younger sister might have a genius level IQ but she rarely remembered to plug in her cell phone. Drumming his fingers on the desk, Parker wondered what had prompted his only sibling to call but not leave a message—she'd never done that before and something about the situation made him more than a little uncomfortable. Scrolling through his messages, he noticed one from Lawton letting them know Cressi had woken up with her vision vastly improved. Parker was almost tempted to wake Carli up to share the news, but the second part of his friend's message made the hair on the back of his neck stand up.

What's up with Liv? She's called twice but no message—not like her.

Parker brought up the tracking program on his computer and just as he suspected, her phone wasn't registering, letting him know she'd let the damned thing go dead again. He hoped like hell she found a man someday who would paddle her sweet ass when she pulled bonehead stunts like this. The little imp had been the light of his life since his parents brought the noisy bundle of pink home from the hospital. Most of his friends complained about their younger brothers and sisters, but Parker had always considered Olivia the best gift his mom and dad had ever given him.

Grabbing his phone, Parker tapped out a quick text to his business partners and team leaders requesting they answer Olivia's calls immediately should they hear from her. Then after a quick note to Lawton and Brodie to let them know how pleased he was to hear about Cressida's improvement, Parker packed up his electronics and set the large case next to the other bags he'd packed earlier. Since Sawyer was accompanying them to London for some well-deserved R&R, he'd offered to pick up all the luggage when he headed out to the airfield early the next morning.

Sliding between the sheets, Parker pulled Carli from her warm spot cuddled against Tristan and smiled at her grumbling. She fit against him perfectly and something inside him seemed to settle just by holding her close. Parker remembered his first big break-up with a girlfriend. He'd been in high school and convinced he'd just lost the woman of his dreams. His dad had found him sitting out on their back deck trying to choke down a glass of whiskey—just because that's what he'd seen guys do in the movies. His dad had shaken his head and warned him against adding a headache to his heartache before handing him one of his favorites—a fresh squeezed cherry limeade.

"I know you're hurting and me telling you that in the great scheme of things this is a small bump in the road isn't going to mean a damned thing—even though it's true. Someday, years down the road you'll think back on this night and wonder what her name was." Thinking back, Parker had to really dig deep in his memory to bring Becky Blair's name back to the surface. Hell, he hadn't thought about her in years—his dad had been right, he'd all but forgotten the pain he'd felt so acutely that night. The one thing that had stuck with him was the bit of insight his dad had shared as they'd watched the moon move slowly across the sky. He'd never forgotten his dad's words, often wondering if he'd missed something along the way. Hell, he'd slept with a lot of women over the years, but he'd never experienced the *connection* his dad had spoken about that night—until this moment, and now his father's words seemed almost prophetic.

His dad had been gazing out over the meadow behind their country estate, watching the moonlight dance over the water of the lake he'd built because his beautiful wife loved fishing. His dad worshipped his mom, and the feeling was obviously mutual. Parker grew up watching the two of them behave like newlyweds and had been surprised the first time he'd seen a friend's parents fighting like cats and dogs.

Nuzzling his nose into Carli's hair, Parker inhaled the fresh scent of the shampoo they'd used on her earlier. She'd been putty in their hands when he'd massaged her scalp as he'd washed her hair. He found himself content just holding her close and that feeling brought back his dad's words, "Parker, you'll know when you've found your soul mate, she'll be the one who stills all that rages within you just being in your embrace." At seventeen his dad's words had sounded like Shakespearean bunk, but now, he understood every word.

Parker felt himself sinking into sleep, something that rarely happened for at least an hour after he'd gone to bed, probably another credit he could give to the sweet woman who kept pressing her lovely ass against him. Letting the curtain of sleep fall over him washed the day's concerns from his mind and contentment warmed the last fleeting moments of consciousness.

LIV PACED BACK and forth on the tarmac in front of the short stairway leading up into T.E.G.'s corporate jet. She'd paid the enormous man standing guard at the gate a substantial amount of money for the chance to speak with the pilot. God, she'd hoped it would be Lawton Hill, but as she'd approached Olivia had watched three men board the plane, two in pilots' uniforms and neither of them were the man she'd hoped to see. This really was her best hope for getting out of the country for a few weeks, so she had to figure out a new plan—fast. Thinking back over the past six months, Liv regretted overlooking several warning signs. She'd rationalized all the times she'd felt uncomfortable as regret for not leveling with her family about what she was working on, and now she was paying for it. *Damn it, Parker is going to blow a gasket.*

She needed time to figure out who had breached the secure programs on her files and made it appear as though she'd shared her conclusions with unauthorized agency contacts both domestic and foreign—hell, they'd basically made it look like she'd betrayed her country. She was certain they hadn't used their planted information yet, but it was only a matter of time before they leveraged it against her—what she didn't know was what they'd be asking for in return.

Double fuck a duck, she'd stepped into it big this time. And damn it, she'd been trying to call her brother and his business partners for hours, she didn't call Tristan because his schedule was so odd she hated disturbing him at work and she never knew when he was sleeping. The one time she had called him, the woman's screams in the background had been so loud people all around her had stared in complete mortification. *Yeah, try explaining that to a table of little old ladies with blue bouffants at the local coffee shop.*

She hadn't left messages simply because she didn't trust that it was safe to do so—she knew all too well how little security there was in anything electronic. Damn it all to hell, she knew her older brother was going to be pissed, but stowing away on the T.E.G. jet really was her last and best chance to buy some time. Decision made, Liv tiptoed up the stairs quickly and moved to the back of the luxurious aircraft. She stuffed her bags behind one of the overstuffed leather sofas before slipping into the smaller bedroom. The closet in the spare bedroom wasn't large, but it was empty. Sliding to the floor, Liv leaned her head back against the wall and breathed a sigh of relief.

How had her life spun so far out of control? The enormity of her situation finally started to dawn on her as the adrenaline she'd been running on for the past thirty-six hours started to fade, Liv felt the first tear slide down her cheek. She didn't ordinarily let herself get sucked into anything resembling self-pity—there just wasn't any point, she might live in DC now, but she'd been raised in Texas. It didn't matter if you'd grown up on a ranch or in the city, everybody in her home state knew the drill...*Suck it up and do what you need to do. If you get bucked off, shake the dust off and go again.*

Letting the tears stream down her cheeks, Liv remembered the guard at the gate mentioning Tristan was accompanying her brother on this trip. She sent up a silent prayer that Tristan would be the one to use this bedroom—he'd be able to talk Parker out of tossing her out at thirty thousand feet...*hopefully*. Well, at least *he* wouldn't yell at her...*probably*.

SAWYER HUGHES WATCHED as the young woman paced outside T.E.G.'s Gulfstream. She'd paid another member of T.E.G.'s security team an absurd amount of money to speak with the pilot, but she hadn't made any attempt to board the plane. When he reviewed the outside security feed, he noticed her making her way across the tarmac as he and the flight team had boarded, but she'd stopped and frowned, telling him whoever she'd been hoping to talk to hadn't been among them. After Parker's message last night, Sawyer had searched the internet for information about Olivia Daniels and been more than a little impressed by what he'd learned. Even though he couldn't see her face now that she'd pulled up her hood to fend off the cool breeze, Sawyer was sure the woman he'd caught just a glimpse of on the tape was indeed Olivia Daniels. The question was, why was one of the country's youngest nuclear physicists sneaking up the steps bags in hand. As he stepped out from the office behind the cockpit, he saw her stuff her bags behind a sofa and slip into the smaller of the two bedrooms.

Since Parker had alerted the team to answer his sister's calls immediately and to accommodate her in any way they could, Sawyer wasn't in a hurry to confront her. Something about the way she'd moved had tipped him off to her fear—and the wave of protectiveness washing over him stopped him cold for several seconds. He finally shook off the feeling, attributing it to the fact she was Parker's sister, and even though Sawyer didn't need the money, he enjoyed working for T.E.G. Sawyer had joined the military as an act of rebellion, but he'd quickly fallen in love with the discipline—something that had been completely lacking in his privileged background.

Growing up in mansions with well-paid, but disinterested nannies providing his only supervision, Sawyer had gotten into plenty of trouble. His parents were nice enough people, but their busy lives left them little time or inclination to raise a son who took no interest in any of the family enterprises. Anastasia Rothschild Hughes might have given birth to him, but she'd paid him very little attention after that. Coming from one of the nation's oldest moneyed families she'd shown an early aptitude in several of her family's business interests, including finance, mining, and energy. It had been her work in the later that had brought her to the attention of Sawyer's father, Charles Hughes. Hughes Oil was one of the largest energy companies in the world and the shipping side of business his dad had inherited was almost as financially viable.

When Sawyer had been seventeen, his father had sent him down to the docks in New York City to work, hoping exposure to that side of the business would spark some interest in his wayward son. Sawyer had certainly learned a lot—but not what his dad had intended. His shaggy blond hair and bright green eyes had made him a favorite with the local ladies—it had been during that time he'd been introduced to BDSM, and he'd certainly seen the darker side of the lifestyle first.

Meeting Parker and Tristan years later had been a fluke, he'd sat down next to them at a bar and overheard enough of their conversation to know they were having trouble purchasing the building they wanted for a club they planned to start. Sawyer had engaged the two men in conversation and then offered to help them make the purchase—they hadn't needed his money, but they had needed his family's connections. It had only taken one phone call for Sawyer to cement his new friendships. He'd left the next day for what turned out to be an extended deployment, but he kept in touch with both Parker and Tristan via email, and by the time he returned, The Knight's Club was the hottest ticket in town. Within a few months, Sawyer had become friends with the other two Knights as well, and working for them was something he did just because he enjoyed it.

When he saw Parker ascending the stairs with a sleeping woman in his arms, Sawyer decided to wait to mention his sister's presence—after all, it wasn't as if Parker was going to throw her off the plane. Nodding to his friends as they secured their sleepy treasure in her seat, Sawyer retrieved Ms. Daniels' cash from their man at the gate—why she'd seemed so desperate to speak to the pilot and then failed to do so was another mystery he'd like to solve. By the time Sawyer stepped out of the office after takeoff, Tristan and Parker were moving Carli to the larger of the two bedrooms and Parker had waved him off when he started their way. He didn't expect to see them again until they landed in London, which left him to find out exactly what was up with their pretty little stowaway.

Chapter Thirteen

CARLI WAS BARELY cognizant of her surroundings until she felt the unmistakable rumble of a jet taxiing down the runway. It didn't matter how often she flew, she always had the same reaction—even before it was time to board she would get so sleepy she could barely keep her eyes open and she usually slept the entire flight. When she had questioned her doctor about it, he'd described it as a coping mechanism for anxiety and told her to be grateful her mind hadn't come up with something far worse. Floating in that blissful state between fully asleep and consciousness, Carli remembered the men being surprised she hadn't fought them when they'd told her they were leaving today for London.

Aside from her sister, Carli had no real reason to stay in New York City, and once she'd learned Cressi's eyesight was returning, getting out of the country had seemed like a great plan. Knowing Cressida was in the loving hands of two men who adored her made leaving possible. She'd been secretly relieved to have a chance to get away with Tristan and Parker—thinking about returning to her apartment alone made her more than a little uncomfortable. Carli wasn't always the tower of strength her sister believed her to be, knowing the space had already been compromised once left her terrified it would happen again.

Cressida was also mistaken in her belief their father had always taken Carli's side—she'd just been more ruthless in manipulating him. She'd always marveled at the fact he'd failed to love the daughter most like the wife he'd adored—it still baffled her.

Snuggling down further into her seat, Carli let her mind go blank—she was tired of constantly having to consider each and every possible angle of every situation. And continually being forced to try to determine who was a friend and who was a foe, drained her. There were moments when the only person in the world she trusted implicitly was her sister. She loved Cressida with everything in her, but there was a small part of her that was totally envious of what the little imp had found with Lawton and Brodie. What would it be like to know the men in your life believed you were the center of the universe? Up until a few days ago, Carli hadn't held out much hope that she'd ever find that kind of happiness, but now she couldn't help but wonder if she'd been too cynical. As the dark cloud of sleep rolled over her, Tristan's and Parker's faces moved through her mind—was it too much to hope for?

PARKER LOOKED DOWN at Carli after tucking a soft blanket around her, leaning down he pressed a gentle kiss against the smooth skin of her forehead. A picture flashed through his mind where he was doing the same thing, but this time the hands tucking in the blanket were much older showing the passage of time, and the forehead beneath his lips was riddled with the wrinkles of laugh lines and a life well lived. A week ago it would have terrified him—today it sent a wave of warmth through his chest and he felt his breath catch.

Watching as Tristan leaned down kissing her cheek, Parker knew his friend had already decided she was the one, but Parker would need longer to be sure she understood everything they would expect of her. "She's so beautiful, inside and out. I can't tell you how thrilled I am that she has decided to try. And to be honest, I think she'll find everything she's been looking for in the lifestyle."

"I'm convinced her submission runs even deeper than Cressida's, but I'm even more convinced she's going to fight it when push comes to shove." Tristan nodded but didn't comment. "I know what you're thinking, you know." The man who could talk a blue streak when he was trying to make a point, simply raised his brow as they settled into their own seats preparing for takeoff.

Parker shook his head, "You think I'm fighting you on this and I'm not—well, not really. I'm just not convinced she fully understands what she's getting into. Hell, according to my sister, I'm a controlling bastard on a good day." When Tristan laughed, Parker glared, "The only reason she didn't say the same thing about you is she's about two-thirds afraid of you. She knows I love her so she's safe—mostly, from me. But the beautiful little trouble magnet sleeping so peacefully over there doesn't have that sibling safety net—she's an international celebrity for God's sake, how will either of us cope with the strain that puts on a relationship. Men will look at her and I'll want to beat my chest and scream 'Mine!' and I think we both know how well that's going to work out."

Tristan laughed, but Parker knew he'd made his point, "I think that confidence and security will come to you both with time. This is very new and perhaps she won't enjoy the lifestyle as much as I believe she will. Truthfully, I think her kink is darker than Cressida's, but we'll have to wait and see. And as much as I hate sounding like a sappy song from the 70's, we've only just begun. I think you are expecting too much, too soon."

Parker felt the jet level off as they hit cruising speed and altitude just as the lights telling them to stay seated blinked off. "Probably. Let's get her settled in the back, I'd like to see if we can't ease some of her anxiety about flying." They'd both noted the change in Carli as soon as they'd mentioned their plans to fly out today. He'd been pleasantly surprised when she didn't argue with them, but more than a little concerned when she'd barely been able to stay awake long enough to eat the meal he'd set in front of her. By the time they'd gotten her down to the car, she'd been nodding off again—but they'd finally asked enough questions that she'd reluctantly admitted this was her usual response to air travel. It made him shudder thinking about how unsafe the situation was for her. Sure, she had a team of people with her, but with one of that team their prime suspect, he wasn't convinced she was safe in their care. Until they could help her overcome her extreme reaction to flying, he wanted to be sure either he or Tristan went with her.

As they moved down the short hallway to the larger bedroom, Sawyer stepped out of the plane's small office and headed their way. Parker looked up and shook his head, "If it isn't earthshattering or urgent—handle it. I'd rather not be disturbed unless it is something you absolutely cannot handle."

Sawyer seemed to stop and consider what Parker had said—and something about that seemed a bit *off* to Parker, but he finally nodded, "I'll handle it for now and we'll confer just before landing." Parker wasn't sure why they needed to discuss it before landing, but shrugged off his concern and slipped into the bedroom—he had more important matters to attend to.

SAWYER SLIPPED SILENTLY inside the small bedroom surprised to find it dark and empty. Moving to the attached washroom, he was even more puzzled to find it vacant as well. Turning back to leave, he noticed the closet door slightly ajar and knew he'd found her hiding place. Nothing he'd read in Olivia Daniels' bio led him to believe she was specially trained, but he wasn't willing to take the chance, especially since she wouldn't be expecting a stranger. Pulling the door open slowly he scanned the small space before finding her curled up in the back corner almost hidden from view thanks to her dark clothing.

Pushing the door fully open let the soft light from the bedroom filter into the closet highlighting the petite bundle of mischief sleeping so soundly she had yet to realize she was no longer alone. If she belonged to him, she wouldn't be sitting comfortably for a few days—what the hell was she thinking sneaking onto a jet without verifying who was going to be onboard or where it was headed? Before he could wake her, she shifted allowing the light to fall softly on her tear-streaked face—and Sawyer felt like he'd been kicked in the chest. The dark circles under her eyes let him know she'd obviously been running on empty—hell, no wonder she'd fallen asleep. But what had her so spooked she'd been willing to take such a huge chance?

He'd planned to spend some time interviewing her before getting some rest himself, but now he felt as if he should let her sleep for a while first. At his first touch she came up fighting. Turns out the little imp had a hell of a left hook—which, lucky for him landed dead center in the middle of his chest. She pulled her fist back cradling it against her own chest and moaned, "Damn it you scared a year off my life, and what the hell...are you a cyborg or something?" She tunneled her fingers into the front of his shirt and tugged on the hair sprinkled over his chest.

"Jesus Christ, imp—stop that." He'd wrapped his hand around her dainty wrist, fingers pressing against her pulse point. When her eyes met his, Sawyer heard her whisper-soft gasp as her pulse rate ratcheted substantially. He was grateful he hadn't been the only one affected, hell, it felt like he'd taken a roundhouse kick to the side of the head. "Come on, sweetness, let's get you out of this damned closet."

When he started to lift Olivia to her feet, she pulled back, "But you don't know me—why are you being nice? I've stowed away on this jet, what will the owners say?" *Damn, woman, really? You don't think we knew you were aboard?*

"Well, Olivia, I was notified when you paid one of T.E.G. Security's men to speak with the pilot. You then evidently changed your mind because you snuck aboard stashing two bags behind a sofa before hiding in this closet where I found you fast asleep." Brushing the pad of his finger under her eye, he softened his tone, "Sleep I'd say you need desperately. Now, we can talk now or after you rest, your choice. But, imp—we *are* going to talk."

He watched her blue eyes fill with tears and her shoulders sag, whatever weight she was carrying had finally become too much. Sighing, he pulled her against his chest just as the first sob bubbled to the surface. Wrapping his arms around her made him realize how petite she was—which was absolutely amazing considering her brother was fucking huge. Between gulping sobs, she managed to surprise him—not something that happened often, "I don't even know your name." Sawyer managed to hold back his laughter, but just barely. The absurdity of the one thing she'd picked out to focus on wasn't lost on him.

"Sawyer. My name is Sawyer Hughes, Olivia. Now, what's it going to be? Talk now or later?"

"I just can't do it now...I have nothing left. I haven't slept longer than a half hour at a time since—what day is it?" Without giving him time to answer, she pushed right on through waving off her own question, "For a long damned time—don't tell Tristan I said that or he'll give me the evil eye. I hate that look, Parker does it too, but I've had a lot of practice ignoring *him*." Jesus, Joseph, and sweet Mother Mary, the woman was making him dizzy just trying to keep up with her random thoughts. "Anyway, I haven't gotten any Stage 4 sleep for too long—and I only cry when I'm deprived of Serotonin. I love that sweet little neurotransmitter—maybe I should have gone into neurology instead, maybe people wouldn't be after me then...because nobody chases neurologists, right?"

"Imp, you need to stop talking right now. If you continue, we'll be talking for quite a long time and I agree that you really aren't ready for that conversation just yet." He leaned down, and scooped her up in his arms and walked to the small washroom, "Can you undress by yourself?"

"Undress? Why would I do that? I don't think I have any nightclothes—good girls don't sleep naked." When he just stared at her, she laughed, "Figures, you're one of Parker's friends, right? Yep, bossy. Got it." When he set her on her feet, she swayed but caught herself before he needed to steady her. She met his gaze straight on and frowned, "Wait. Did you say Sawyer *Hughes*? As in Hughes Oil…Hughes Shipping…and a zillion other ventures? Why are you working with Parker—you surely don't need the money?" When he smiled, she groaned, "Well fuck me, this just gets worse and worse."

"Careful, imp—Tristan isn't the only one with an aversion to hearing women curse." He watched her eyes widen, he wasn't sure if she was reacting to his change of tone or his words of warning—perhaps both. "Take a quick shower, you'll sleep better. I'll find you something to wear, even though I want to go on record as disagreeing with your assessment about sleeping naked." They'd been standing close enough in the small bathroom that he'd been able to watch her eyes dilate and the pulse at the base of her slender neck kick up substantially. He stepped back before he answered the pleading look in her eyes and kissed her. Hell, kissing would lead very quickly to fucking. And even though he'd like nothing more than to ravage her, he wasn't about to take advantage of her and at this point informed consent would be questionable at the very least.

He returned a few minutes later with one of his own shirts in hand, knowing it was much too large for her, but something about the opportunity to see her—all warm, damp, and flushed from her shower wearing his shirt had been too much to resist. When she stepped into the room, he felt as if all the air had been sucked out of the room. He wasn't going to deny he'd already noticed how beautiful she was, but the woman facing him now gave new meaning to the word gorgeous. Guessing her height at approximately five foot three, he was surprised to see long, tan legs topped by a plush deep blue bath towel that made her blue eyes sparkle with color reminding him of the

Caribbean Sea. She'd dried her hair so the long blonde strands fell in a shiny curtain down her back just brushing the top of her ass cheeks. Her face was scrubbed clean leaving her high cheekbones highlighted a beautiful shade of pink. In a word—she was stunning.

When she held out her hand for the shirt Sawyer shook his head, stepping closer he used his finger to make a motion for her to turn around. Leaning down over her shoulder, he spoke against the warm shell of her ear, "Drop the towel, imp."

Chapter Fourteen

LAWTON HILL LEANED back against the living room sofa and watched Cressida bounce excitedly into the room. She'd woken up early this morning to find her eyesight vastly improved, but a morning of excited chatter and constant movement had diminished her progress considerably by lunch. Their insistence that she rest again had been met with just enough resistance to earn her a couple of solid swats before she'd finally returned to their shared bedroom to sleep.

Brodie had drawn the short straw and gone to the club to help in Tristan's and Parker's absence—when the four of them started the club several years earlier, they'd all agreed that at least one of them would be present anytime the club was open for business. It was a policy designed to protect all of their interests and had paid off on several occasions. Grateful for the chance to spend some quality time alone with his wife, Lawton closed his laptop before she had a chance to notice the email he'd been reading.

Dale Roberts had once again sent him a large file of information about the woman suspected of attacking Cressida. Lawton had verified all the information in the first file and would do the same again, but he had to admit, he was more than a little impressed with the man's ability to ferret out information. As angry as he was at the asshat who'd essentially set Cressida up a couple months earlier, he was reluctantly coming to the conclusion the computer wizard might actually be useful. Shoving thoughts of the man who was still obsessed with his wife aside, Lawton held open his arms and was thrilled when Cressida rushed to settle on his lap.

"You did that without even a moment's hesitation so I'm assuming your vision is clear once again." Even though it hadn't actually been a question, she'd detected it in his tone, nodding enthusiastically.

"It is *almost* normal except for distances which are still a little fuzzy. But that strange halo around things and the feeling I was looking through a mist all the time is much better. I'm so excited, I can hardly wait to tell Brodie and Carli. What were you working on? Anything I can help with? I miss working, you know. When are you going to let me come back?" Typical Cressida—firing off questions as fast as her mind could tick them off and that was saying a lot.

"We've had this discussion, baby. We're asking you to develop the new philanthropic division for Templar Enterprises, Group. As our wife, having you work for us directly would be a violation of the rules we've insisted everyone else abide by—not something we want to do. This expansion is something we'd talked about for a while, and it would be a significant promotion for you. The renovations have already been started, so our office suite will be accessible from yours." Since she hadn't been downstairs, he would leave out some of the more interesting aspects of the renovation. The area behind all three of their offices had formed an odd shaped space they'd converted into a small sitting room. No one walking through would notice the *specialized furnishings*, but each piece served more than one purpose. It was definitely an executive's dream for a playroom—elegant kink.

"You have a really devious grin on your face, you know. What's that about? Did you paint my office some funky color or something? Oh, fu...n times, you didn't paint it green did you?" He wanted to groan at her quick save, she usually remembered to clean up her language with him when he didn't mind nearly as much as Brodie did, the man was a real stickler for protocol. But without fail she let the words fly when Brodie was nearby—they'd actually started to wonder if she wasn't doing it on purpose.

"No, baby, we remembered you didn't want anything green. I think you'll be happy with the results, after all Jeffrey designed the entire space." He'd even helped them find all the specialty pieces for the playroom, but Lawton didn't feel the need to mention that particular piece of information. Since Jeffrey was a sub, he'd consulted with his long-time Master, and Marco had known exactly what would please a couple of experienced sexual Dominants. And judging from the text message Lawton had gotten earlier, working together on the kinky project had evidently infused the two men's relationship with a renewed passion since they were currently enjoying a very hot scene on one of the club's largest public stages.

Cuddling closer, her words wafted softly over the side of his neck and he wanted to groan at the sensation, "You're the best, every single day I thank God for you and Brodie." When he snorted a laugh, she added, "Okay, maybe not every day—but most days, that's for sure." Cressida was never going to be a perfect submissive—her fiery personality and inability to sensor her opinions when she was frustrated assured them she'd be spending a lot of time draped over his lap. He could certainly think of worse ways to spend time than warming her ivory ass cheeks until they were a lovely blush pink.

What she didn't know was how attractive her rebellious streak was—both men loved that spark of defiance because it meant she challenged them, something that had rarely happened before they'd hired her as their executive assistant. In Lawton's opinion, one of the downsides of extreme wealth was the fact you rarely knew what people *really* thought because they tended to tell you what you wanted to hear rather than the unvarnished truth. From the beginning, Cressida had been honest—often to the point of being borderline rude and insubordinate, something she'd learned to rein in professionally if not personally.

"As much as I'm enjoying having you curled up in my lap like a very soft, warm kitten—I'm curious as to why you are dressed." She knew the rules, when they were alone, she was supposed to be naked unless they'd given her specific instructions otherwise. Her training had been completely derailed when she'd been injured, but it was time to reestablish their roles.

He heard her soft inhalation of breath before she sat back to look into his face, "I guess I had forgotten since things have been so crazy. And, I thought you had changed your mind about having me as a submissive since...well, since you have kind of ignored me *that way* since I fell down those damned stairs."

Everything inside him shifted, what the hell was she talking about? "Explain."

She blinked several times and Law wondered for a few seconds if she was trying to pull back her emotions or if she didn't know how to articulate the insecurity he'd heard underlying her comment. "You…well, neither of you have seemed…well, you haven't seemed particularly interested in going back to the way things were, except for the punishments—you seem pretty keen on keeping those."

"Cressida, what about your accident do you think changed our sexual kink? And do you really think you would be happy with a vanilla lifestyle?" He already knew the answer to the last question but he wanted to make sure *she* recognized it as well. When her chin dropped to her chest he used two fingers to lift her face back to his, "Don't hide from me, baby. We need to talk this out. This isn't how I saw our time alone playing out, but we need to get to the heart of this problem right now. I don't want this between us."

"It's not that you haven't been loving…you've just been different. Even if my eyesight hadn't come back, I wouldn't have wanted this—distance." Well, that explained a lot. He and Brodie had discussed her increasingly antagonistic attitude, wondering if she was reacting to the uncertainty of her condition, or if she was missing the intimacy of kink. Now it looked like they had their answer, their little sub had gone to a lot of trouble to find out if the lifestyle was for her and it didn't look like she was going to give it up easily. *Thank God.*

"Well, let me assure you, nothing has changed, so, sweet wife—the clock is ticking. Why are you still dressed?"

OLIVIA SHIVERED AT Sawyer's command to drop the towel and shut down the part of her brain that knew it wasn't a good idea to set a precedence of compliance—God forbid he should get the idea she was cooperative. But the soft brush of his warm breath over her ear melted her resistance and she felt her fingers open letting the towel slide to the floor. "Good girl. You're beautiful, Olivia. Has anyone ever told you? Did you believe them?" Her entire body shuddered as she reacted to his words. Without even looking down, Liv knew her nipples were drawn up into tight buds reaching out for the touch they'd been denied for so long. She could almost feel her pussy lips swelling and the moisture flooding her sex in hopes of easing a man's way into her body. "Your body is speaking very loudly, imp, and trust me when I tell you mine is completely on board. But you need to rest and then we need talk, so we're not going there right now."

Under any other circumstances, Liv might have felt a sting of rejection at Sawyer's comments, so she was surprised when all she felt was relief. She knew her judgement was not at all what it should be because she was running on empty, and the truth was all she wanted was to collapse onto the bed and fall into a sleep coma. Sawyer slid the shirt up her arms and then turned her so she was facing him as he fastened the middle three buttons. When she reached up to finish the others he shook his head closing his hand gently over hers. He led her to the bed and once he'd tucked her in he stood to leave. "Wait. Could you stay, please…just until I fall asleep? I know I'm safe, but…"

SAWYER PRESSED HIS fingers over her lips and smiled, "No need to explain. Don't ever be afraid to ask for what you need, Olivia. Men aren't mind readers, despite what we may lead you to believe, communication is always the key." He sat down, leaning his back against the headboard, stroking his fingers softly over the gentle curves of her face. Her soft sigh of contentment let him know how much she enjoyed his touch—he'd learned a long time ago how effective light touches to the face could be when trying to calm an anxious submissive.

Even though her breathing had leveled out indicating she'd already fallen asleep, he stayed for several more minutes simply because he was enjoying the feel of her soft skin beneath his fingertips, and holy fucking hell the woman was straight up gorgeous. Parker Daniels might have a supermodel in his bed, but the man's little sister would give Carli Walker a run for her money in looks—not to mention from what he'd read, Olivia was ridiculously academically gifted, making him wonder once again what kind of trouble she was in that would prompt her to hide on a flight out of the country. Unable to resist, he leaned down and pressed a soft kiss to her forehead, "Sleep well, imp. Whatever has sent you running into our care can't hurt you now."

Moving slowly in hopes he wouldn't disturb her much needed rest, he frowned when she started to cry softly in her sleep, whispering something about not knowing and it not being her fault. *What the hell have you gotten yourself into, sweetheart?*

Chapter Fifteen

TRISTAN HAD ALWAYS been a light sleeper so he'd awakened as soon as Carli began to stir. He heard her swear softly when she shifted—*yes, love, I'll bet you are sore in places you'd forgotten were there.* She tried to roll over, but he and Parker had her sandwiched tightly between them—she wasn't going anywhere until one of them allowed it. Tristan was willing to bet Carli hadn't ever experienced the kind of marathon sex they'd shared last night, hell, it'd been a workout for all three of them. He'd lost track of how many times they'd made her come, but she'd been out cold by the time they'd finished washing all the evidence of their lovemaking from between her slender thighs. Not wanting her to be uncomfortable while she slept, they'd also dried her soft skin before tucking her between them.

When she tried to sit up, Tristan's arm tightened around her, his hand cupping her breast in a possessive grip that was firm without being painful. *"Mon amour,* where do you think you are going?"

"To the bathroom, if I can get myself out of here." Struggling against his hold, she quickly discovered it was an exercise in frustration.

Parker leaned over to seal his lips over hers stilling her movements. Tristan watched as the kiss that had started out as a chaste peck quickly turned deep, hot, and possessive. When he finally pulled back Parker flashed her a smile Tristan recognized, he called it Parker's "big bad wolf" grin—because it was the same one his friend always had just before he declared he was going to eat a little sub. "Princess, you don't get out of bed without notifying one of us."

"But we're on a plane. I'm safe here."

"It's not about safety, it's about protocol. You agreed to give the lifestyle a shot—and this is just one of the elements. And for the record, we will want to know you are safe at all times—it won't be up to you to decide when the rules should be applied and when they should not."

Tristan used the tip of his tongue to draw a slow circle below her ear before whispering, "Not needing to overthink everything is actually one of the perks of being a submissive. All those troubling little decisions you usually struggle with? They all disappear, freeing your attention for the things that really matter."

For a few seconds it sounded wonderful, but then her brain turned back on, "Wait a minute, are you saying I have to ask permission to use the bathroom? Because I'm telling you right now, that's a deal breaker. Oh dear God, does Cressida have to beg to pee? Holy crap on a cracker, where's my damned phone? Shit, we're still in the air, aren't we? Boy oh boy, this is completely flipping insane. I'm totally out, now. Ask permission to pee, what kind of third world patriarchal bullshit is that?"

Tristan went completely still glaring at Parker over Carli's shoulder as his friend tried desperately to refrain from bursting out in laughter like a blasted hyena. *Mon cher,* I do believe we have a problem." The look on her face changed quickly from indignant defiance to dawning realization, and then to worry. "Yes, you have good cause for concern, sweet sub. Even though we weren't technically in a scene—your intentional misinterpretation of what your Dom was explaining, your disrespectful response, and your cursing are all adding up very quickly." He felt a shudder move through her and now he was the one who wanted to smile because her response had been perfect. God in heaven she was going to be a joy to train, and he hoped it took the rest of their lives for her to get it right.

Parker scooted out of the way and held out his hand to her, "Come on, princess. Go on to the bathroom, Master Tristan and I want to discuss the best way to deal with your outburst. Don't be too long, though, or we'll know you are stalling—and that will not serve you well." Tristan had to give the man credit, he'd pulled that off perfectly, even when Tristan knew he was fighting not to die laughing at the predicament she'd gotten herself into.

As soon as the door closed behind her, Parker grinned, "I swear sometimes I think she is her own worst enemy. But since it serves our interests this time, I'm having trouble working up any real frustration about it. I think we should use it as a teachable moment and torture her a bit. Orgasm denial is always a great way to remind subs that their cooperation reaps rewards while their misbehavior does not." Tristan agreed, hell she'd come during previous spankings so it was hard to see how that would be a punishment for her unless they upped the stakes a lot and she certainly wasn't ready for that level of intensity yet.

"Good plan, though once we get to the estate, we need to make sure she understands exactly how it's going to be, because I think we all need to know now if this isn't going to work—before we get into it any further." Tristan knew he was already in too deep, he'd be crushed if she walked away, but there might still be a chance to save Carli and

Parker the same heartache. Parker looked at him, the unvoiced question in his eyes—*Yes, I'd have to walk away if she decides the D/s lifestyle isn't for her.* He'd promised himself years ago when he found the right woman, nothing would stand in his way, but he couldn't expect her to live a life she wasn't comfortable with, he had to be true to himself as well.

When she stepped back into the room, her cheeks were flushed and even though it was easy to see the hesitance in her body language, her eyes were bright with anticipation. He studied her closely as she took first one and then two steps into the room. It was obvious she wasn't sure what they expected from her—*yes, sweet girl, waiting for our instructions is exactly what you should do, but you shouldn't look so uncertain*, and that was their fault. She'd had very little training, so they'd need to proceed with any punishments very carefully. If she only saw the negative side of the lifestyle there would be no reason for her to want to continue.

As Carli's Doms it was their responsibility to introduce her to as many aspects of the lifestyle as she was comfortable with—and to make sure she always knew she had the ability to stop any scene just by using her safe word. Tristan used his finger to beckon her closer, "Come here, *mon cher.*" When she was standing right in front of him, he stoked the backs of his fingers down the top curve of her breast, watching her nipples draw up into tight peaks and her areolas darken as blood rushed to sensitize the entire area. "We're going to do things a little differently this time, sweet sub. But before we start, let's review—what's your safe word, Carli?"

"Red, sir. Yellow if I need a timeout or have a question." Her voice had taken on the slightly breathless quality he'd notice accompanied her arousal so he gave her a small smile of approval. The plan was to reinforce the behaviors they liked whenever they could—a sub who understood what was expected of them was far more compliant than one who always felt as if they were floundering around in the dark.

"Good girl. Don't forget to use them. Now, tell us what you did wrong." After her spot-on recounting of her earlier behavior, he tied a silk scarf around her eyes and then he and Parker tied their beautiful woman to the bed. Looking down on her, Tristan marveled at her reaction. Up to now, they'd only bound either her hands or her feet, never both—but now she'd been secured spread-eagled on the bed. Someday soon, they'd use silencing headphones to block out her ability to anticipate by sound, but for now, they all needed to be able to communicate as clearly as possible.

"Princess, for this scene there are a few basic rules. First and most importantly, you are not allowed to come."

She groaned and the scent of her honey immediately flooded the room. "I'm not sure I know how to prevent it—I mean that isn't a skill I ever anticipated needing, you know?" Parker leaned down giving her pussy a mild swat. "Hey, holy cats that hurt, that's a pretty sensitive spot you know—particularly after a marathon round with a couple of sex machines." The last part had been spoken so softly he might not have heard her if he hadn't been watching her so closely. *Sex machines, huh? Well, sweet woman of ours, you haven't seen anything yet.*

PARKER THANKED HIS lucky stars Carli wasn't able see their

reaction to her comment. Hell, he figured they'd both puffed up like a couple of toads at her remark. His mom had always insisted most of the male population's pride was centered below the waist, he had always considered her comments as sarcasm, but he might have to reconsider and revise. Running his finger under the bindings, Parker asked, "Are these too tight, princess?"

"No, sir." Her short, succinct answer didn't surprise him—he'd learned over the years, taking away a subs ability to be distracted by everything happening around them went a long way to center their attention on the here and now.

"I want to remind you that you *do not* have permission to come. If you do, we'll begin again. And, princess—we can do this for the rest of this flight without breaking a sweat." Okay, that was probably not entirely true, breaking a sweat was definitely in their future.

"I know you don't understand how pleasure can be used as punishment, *mon amōre*—but you will. Don't come." At Tristan's nod, Parker fit his mouth directly over the top of her sex, sucking hard on her clit. At the same time, Tristan had covered the peak of one breast, sucking the nipple into a hard peak so he could slide the clamp on before giving her other breast the same treatment. Since they'd left her very little room for movement, Carli's attempts to arch her back were futile, adding to her frustration.

Parker felt the engorged lips of her labia start to tremble, a sign he'd come to recognize. How could she be so close to release this quickly? Pulling back, he asked, "Princess? Have you forgotten already?" He watched as she took several gulping breaths trying to calm herself, but the flush covering her entire body wasn't fading letting him know she wasn't making much progress pulling herself back from the edge. As untrained as she was, he didn't expect her to be able to hold her release off for long, but he had expected her to last more than ninety seconds.

Tristan was leaning back watching her closely, when he looked up at Parker the grin he flashed was almost feral. "Perhaps this will help her remember why she is in this particular predicament." He slid the nipple clamp on so quickly she hadn't had time to react. Tristan hadn't tightened it to the extreme, but she was no doubt feeling a sharp pinch. To her credit, Carli hadn't screamed, but she'd pulled her bottom lip between her teeth and was biting down so hard he was worried she might draw blood.

"Don't bite your lip, princess. We don't want you battered and bruised when we land. And I do believe Master Tristan has plans for your lovely mouth in the very near future." The trembling in her sex had subsided so Parker began pumping his fingers in and out of her channel curving them every few passes to press against the spongy area of the G-spot. He kept the pattern random so she couldn't anticipate the pleasure. Not having that predictability kept her mind engaged a little longer, and should help her stave off her release while Tristan slid the other clamp into place and hooked the chain between the two jeweled pieces.

"*Mon cher*, you've taken your punishment beautifully so far, and we're very proud of you. Now, let's see if we can push you just a bit further. Open for me." Parker moved to press his cock against her opening at the same time Tristan pressed his own against her lips. In a well-choreographed move, they both pushed forward at the same moment. Tristan hadn't gone in as far as Parker had, assuring him his friend was already fighting his own release.

When Parker felt the first telltale muscle contractions of her vaginal muscles he stilled, fighting the almost overwhelming urge to thrust in mindless abandon until he found his own release. What was it about this woman that made him want to break all of his own rules? He'd never had a problem holding back in order to achieve a goal with a submissive. Delaying their pleasure was one of the best ways to amplify the experience, and he and Tristan had the process down to a near science—until now. Maybe Tristan was right, maybe Carli was the woman they'd been waiting for—God only knew she challenged him on levels he'd never even realized he could be tested. But he wasn't sure how he'd ever be able to deal with her travel schedule—and then there was the issue of his fears for her safety. Could he let her be out of the country for a week or two at a time? *She's going to make me lose my mind.*

CARLI WAS LITERALLY vibrating with unspent energy. Both men had finally found their own releases, shouting her name as they came. And, under normal circumstances, she would have been lost in that moment...but, Carli had been so absorbed in battling back her own orgasm she hadn't been able to enjoy any part of the experience. When they'd finally released her and she had managed to convince them she wasn't experiencing any tingling or lasting effects from being bound or from their torturous nipple clamps, Carli hurried into the small lavatory under the pretense of needing to use the restroom. Once inside, she locked the door, turned on the shower, and let the tears fall.

She felt as if she was drowning in emotions as desperation, rejection, and a soul-deep feeling of stark loneliness tore her usual composure to shreds. Carli knew Tristan and Parker had been making a point—though at the moment it wasn't entirely within her grasp. All she knew in this moment was that she'd never felt so used and rejected in her entire life. *How did Cressi deal with Dad's rejection all those years?* Carli had never personally experienced this kind of despair before and couldn't imagine how her younger sister had survived it.

The lack of a *connection* during sex had completely changed the way her body had reacted. As soon as both men had reached their climaxes, her body had turned to stone and her mind had pushed them away in an effort to save her heart any further suffering. The fragile bond they'd been forging was now deeply fractured and she wasn't sure things would ever be the same between the three of them. She'd always felt cherished when they'd made love to her, she'd even felt valued when they'd paddled her because there had still been an emotional connection. But this punishment had been far less emotional—they'd deliberately denied her pleasure while taking their own, making her feel like little more than a vessel they'd used before tossing it aside.

Grabbing a small hand towel from the counter, Carli slid slowly down the slick wall of the shower until she was huddled in the corner. She buried her face in the small cloth hoping to muffle the sounds of the racking sobs that shock her entire body. She didn't know how long she could hide from them—or how she was ever going to face them again, but in this moment the only thing that mattered was letting the warm water wash away as much of the emotional sewage as possible.

Chapter Sixteen

SAWYER LOOKED BACK at the sleeping woman lying so peacefully on the bed and wondered what on earth she'd gotten herself in to, and how her brother was going to react when he found out she was aboard. Once back in the jet's small office, he called the one man he trusted above all others—James Mikels. The two friends had laughed when they both found themselves working for the same group of people despite living on different continents. Sawyer had already been employed by Templar Enterprises Security Division when Tristan Harris' parents began experiencing severe security breaches their staff hadn't been able to resolve. Since Sawyer had known his friend recently retired from SAS he'd arranged a meeting between his friend and the Harris'; Sawyer might have set up the meeting, but his friend had gotten the job all on his own.

Retired SAS members were in high demand as security consultants and James had been one of his agency's best. Members of the SAS were widely considered the best-trained covert operators in the world. Every Special Forces team in existence used training protocols pioneered by the British SAS. Sawyer knew the Harris family was not only thrilled to have hired James, but they all got along so well the fun-loving, aristocratic couple had all but adopted him. William and Mary Elizabeth Harris had become the family

James no longer had, and it hadn't hurt that he reminded them so much of their only son. Both men were tall, always looked as if they'd just returned from a tropical holiday, and both had the same commanding presence. The only difference was their eye color. While both men technically had blue eyes, James's were actually violet—a trait so distinctive he'd been forced to wear colored contacts during most of his missions because people *always* commented on and remembered his eye color.

Sawyer and James met when their teams joined forces on a mission early in their military careers, and during a late night chat they'd discovered a number of mutual interests, including a shared passion for sexual dominance. They'd met in cities all over the world over the years whenever they'd been on leave at the same time, and learned that while they were both well trained—the pleasure they could give a submissive when they worked together was exponentially better than when they worked alone.

"What aren't you telling me, my friend? You're dancing around something and this isn't the time." Sawyer heard the rapid fire tapping of a computer keyboard and then James's low whistle. "Olivia Daniels and Parker Daniels are brother and sister? Are you certain?" Sawyer couldn't hold back his chuckle—hell, he'd wondered the same thing. "Seriously, man—which one of them is adopted? I am absolutely certain what I'm reading simply cannot be accurate." Yeah, Sawyer could sympathize with his friend's confusion.

"Yes, they are full brother and sister, but there is more than a decade between them."

"And a foot in height judging from her file. And I don't even want to speculate on the weight difference. Tell that ugly mugged boss of yours that his sister is far better looking than he could ever hope to be." Sawyer wanted to laugh at his friend's irreverence, for a man raised by parents whose blood was as blue as any had ever been, the prudishness of the aristocracy hadn't seemed to have had much of an impact on James Mikels.

"You can tell him yourself when we get there, I'm sure he'll be fascinated with your assessment. Until then, find out what you can about who she might be running from and why."

There was a long pause before James answered, "I'll call in a few favors and find out what I can, but I'm hesitant to stir murky water too much before we know what's lurking beneath the surface. I assume Parker doesn't know anything about this since you're the one calling." Sawyer didn't answer—he didn't have to, James knew him better than anyone ever had, he'd figure out Sawyer's interest soon enough, if he hadn't already. "Is she a sub?" The question sounded innocent enough, but Sawyer heard the interest lying just below the surface.

"Yes, but I doubt she knows it, and I'll bet you a bottle of Macallan she'll spout all the usual excuses, plus some we probably haven't heard yet. She'd beautiful and brilliant—she's not going to understand the benefits of submission." He'd said more than he should have—damn it, he'd just armed his best friend with far more ammo than he needed. Just as he was ready to end the call a blood-curdling scream followed by a string of cursing that would make any soldier proud filled the air. Snapping out, "Later," he ended the call without waiting for James to answer. He rounded the corner of the small galley just as Parker and Tristan crowded in from the other side.

Carli Walker stood with her hand pressed against her

chest panting as if she'd just run a marathon, "Holy hell, I'm so sorry. I had no idea anyone was in here. I'm—"

"I know who you are—everybody on the planet knows who you are for heaven's sake...you're Carli Walker. The question is what the hell are you doing on the Templar jet with my brother and his kinky crew?"

"Shortcake? We all know why Carli is aboard..."

Carli's detached tone surprised Sawyer when she interrupted Parker, "I'm just a client, and I'm sorry but I didn't catch your name." Sawyer watched the stunned looks on Parker's and Tristan's faces at Carli's description of herself as just a client and wondered what they'd done to fuck up what had appeared to be a very cozy arrangement when the three of them had boarded a couple of hours earlier.

"I'm Olivia Daniels—it's nice to meet you Carli. The big lug standing behind you looking like he just sucked on a lemon is my brother, though I suspect I might not admit that so freely if I knew what he and Prince Tristan have done to cause all this tension. Holy hell, I'm worried the plane's going to burst."

"For a woman with an IQ that makes Mensa membership seem like an insult, you are remarkably inept when it comes to grasping the fact I'm not a prince, short stuff." Tristan's voice was filled with frustration, but Sawyer could also hear the underlying affection. Obviously he'd been dealing with his best friend's little sister long enough to know she was a handful.

"It's Short*cake*—as in Strawberry Shortcake." Turning to Carli, she shrugged, "She was my favorite when I was a kid and since my brother has obviously suffered one too many head injuries playing football and can't come up with anything more contemporary I don't kick up a fuss. Mother insists I humor him—he's her favorite, you know...it's pathetic, really." Sawyer saw Carli's lip twitch at Olivia's antics, and he could only hope he was doing a better job of hiding his amusement because Parker Daniels looked like his head was getting ready to rotate on his shoulders. Sawyer would bet Olivia had been giving her brother fits forever, but the affection between them was easy to see. If Parker was smart, he'd thank his sister later for defusing what had obviously been a very tense situation with Carli.

Carli shook Olivia's outstretched hand before excusing herself. Tristan surprised Sawyer by being the first to round on the petite bundle of trouble standing between them, "Olivia, I'd be very interested to know why you are wearing Sawyer's shirt and from what I can tell—little else, but I need to check on Carli, so I'm leaving you in your brother's capable hands."

"Be careful, Your Highness, I might think you were actually concerned about my honor. But you really should give me more credit than to think I'd shag a man I'd only just met. Now, go see if you can undo whatever you two Neanderthals did to put that look of pain in her pretty eyes."

Sawyer felt himself stiffen when the other man leaned forward and kissed Olivia on the forehead, "We'll handle whatever's brought you here, sweetheart. Now, be a good girl and talk to your brother before he has a stroke." Sawyer didn't realize his fists were clenched tight until he saw Parker glance down and then raise his brow in question. *Don't even ask, because I don't understand it myself.*

An hour later, Olivia had given them a detailed account of the past six months and Parker Daniels was as close to losing it as Sawyer had ever seen him. She'd saved the kicker until the end and judging by her brother's reaction, Olivia had known the effect her pronouncement was going to have. Parker was clearly steamed, "I can't fucking believe you went to work as a spook and didn't bother to mention it. You are a scientist, not a trained operative. Did it occur to you that our government might not give a rat's ass about your safety? That they might be just as corrupt as those they've asked you to spy on? Christ, it took less than six months for you to get into trouble—I think that has to be some kind of world record."

Olivia had remained unfazed by any of her brother's jabs until that moment and Sawyer seethed as he watched the light fade from her eyes before they filled with unshed tears—and now he was pissed. "That's enough, Parker. Olivia did exactly what she should have done, she sought out the people she knew she could trust with her life, *and* she did it without being trained. Personally, I think you ought to be grateful she managed to make it from DC to New Jersey and onto the plane without incident." Sawyer knew his friend was lashing out at his sister because she was available, when his frustration was actually with a situation where he felt out of control, but that didn't excuse the way he'd hurt the young woman who'd run to him for help. *If he wants to talk about records he needs to consider that we've just gone from one damsel in distress to protect to two while flying over the Atlantic—that surely sets some kind of record.*

"Parker, why don't you go check on Carli, hopefully Tristan has managed to talk the two of you out of whatever mess you've managed to get into." Turning his attention to Olivia he continued speaking to Parker, but didn't let his gaze leave hers, "I have a few more questions for Olivia and then I think she needs to rest. The past couple of days have taken a toll and you know as well as I do what exhaustion does to someone's memory. We will need her help if we're going to keep her safe. She needs rest, not your censure."

Parker nodded and moved forward to enfold his sister in his arms before kissing her on top of her blonde head, "I'm sorry, shortcake, I really am thankful you are here and damned impressed you managed it—I just wish you had called me." Sawyer could see the man knew the minute the words passed over his lips that he'd fucked up—she had tried to call, several times if memory served.

"I tried, I really did. I was afraid to leave a message because I wasn't sure I could trust the system wouldn't be compromised. I only turned my phone on for brief periods of time in case they were using it to track me. I tried to call everyone but Tristan, I never know when he's sleeping—but none of you answered my calls." Sawyer's gut clenched at the defeat he heard in her voice as she detailed the efforts she made to find help, and he made a mental note to be sure to add his and James's contact information to her phone as soon as possible.

"I'm sorry, shortcake, you know I'd have moved heaven and earth to get you to a safe place if I'd known. All of us need to sit down and work out a better communication system—and we will when we get to the Harris' estate. But for now, get some rest and don't mind me, I'm just cranky—it's in my job description as your brother."

As apologies went, Sawyer had certainly heard better—and he thought Olivia deserved more, but he kept his opinion to himself. As soon as Parker was out of earshot, Sawyer saw Olivia's shoulders sag. "Well, that went a little better than I thought it might—at least he didn't throw me off the plane."

"You didn't really believe that was an option, did you?" He watched her blink her eyes several times and he knew she was being pushed too far past exhaustion to answer his questions now. "What woke you, imp? You were sleeping so peacefully when I left you."

"You left me." He smiled down at her and pulled her in close, hugging her against his chest. "It was the first time I've actually slept in days, because I felt safe. But my subconscious must have known you were leaving, because I woke up as soon as the door closed behind you. I tried to go back to sleep, but I couldn't shake the feeling I was being watched." He felt her entire body shudder in his arms, hating the fact she'd spent so much time terrified and alone before making her way to them.

Once he'd gotten her settled again, he sat beside her, his back leaned against the headboard as he made arrangements to have Olivia's apartment secured and the rest of her belongings packed and shipped to T.E.G. headquarters in New York. Looking down at the sleeping woman who had curled herself so close her cheek was pressed against his thigh, Sawyer knew his plan for downtime in London was now off the table. Trailing his fingers through Olivia's long blond hair, he smiled when she pressed into his touch. It surprised him how quickly his priorities had shifted, suddenly the break he'd been looking forward to for months didn't seem as important as it had a few hours earlier.

When he saw a new message from James pop up on the screen he opened the window and frowned. The message was short and to the point without being overly informative, telling him his friend was avoiding the damned keyword crawlers that were so helpful when you were the one tracking. *Sending two teams to retrieve packages. Yours is a bigger challenge to transport so I'll accompany. Looking forward to having you stay with me, you'll be able to tell me all about your obstacles in your new job, sounds like it's going to be a while before it's all settled.* The message had been easy for him to decode, but it still raised more questions than it answered. *What have you gotten yourself into, Olivia?*

PARKER STEPPED INTO the bedroom not sure what to expect, but the deafening silence that greeted him was worse than any of the scenarios he'd imagined. Tristan sat in one of the chairs in the attached sitting area, an open book on his lap, but his focus was on the sleeping goddess curled into a fetal position on the bed. The handkerchief clutched tightly in her small hand and the shimmer of salty tear tracks let him know she'd cried herself to sleep—what he didn't know was why his best friend was sitting across the room from her.

Settling into the other chair, Parker looked at Tristan expectantly, worried about the dismal expression on his friend's face. "For the first time since I became a Master, I'm completely baffled. It's as if she's completely disconnected. She is polite, but there is an unmistakable wall of ice between us that wasn't there before we punished her."

One of Parker's worst nightmares had always been finding the perfect woman and then discovering she wasn't well suited for the lifestyle—or worse yet, she'd be attracted to only one of them, forcing them to choose between the woman or their best friend. But to have found a woman he knew was equally attracted to them both, and whose interest in the lifestyle was glaringly obvious, only to have her shut them out without an explanation? *Not happening.*

"I don't know what happened, but I also don't think

the close confines of a plane are the place to explore whatever trigger we unintentionally tripped over. Let's table the discussion until we're alone at the estate. Once the distraction of other people is gone, we'll push her for answers." *Answers she may not even have.*

"We'll be landing in a couple of hours, I've spoken with my parents and everything is ready for us at the estate. We'll be staying in my wing of the house, but the staff is preparing the guest wing for Olivia."

"I'm not sure Sawyer is going to let her out of his sight and I know he was planning to stay with James." Parker knew James had a huge home inside the secured perimeter of the Harris' large estate, so there wouldn't be any concerns about Olivia's safety if she stayed there. The security measures James would have implemented in his own home were undoubtedly more elaborate than what William and Mary Elizabeth would have been comfortable living with. James loved his gadgets, so Parker wasn't worried about Olivia's physical safety if the men opted to keep her close—although he was a bit concerned about her heart. "We'll see how things shape up. James is already doing some of the legwork and I've sent Lawton the information I have." Parker wasn't sure what was happening between his sister and his friend, but it was clear Sawyer had taken on the role of protector. Oddly enough, having another man step up to help watch after Olivia didn't bother him as much as he'd always worried it might. It was going to be interesting to see how things developed with James, it was common knowledge the two men shared their women and hoped to one day share a wife. Parker wasn't sure how Olivia would feel about a non-traditional marriage, and then there was the question of whether or not Olivia would be able to accept Sawyer and

James's kinks. Then shaking his head hoping to clear those images from his mind. Despite the fact he was one of four owners of The Knight's Club, thinking about his sister in a D/s relationship wasn't a place he was willing to go.

Chapter Seventeen

CARLI LOOKED OUT the SUV's window watching the beauty of the English countryside scroll by in fading color as the sun slipped slowly behind the rolling green hills. She'd been surprised when Tristan slid into the seat behind the driver and Parker had taken the passenger seat, obviously she was too accustomed to her security detail leaving her in the backseat alone. There had been a fleet of cars waiting for them and she hadn't missed the fact Olivia had been hustled quickly into a large SUV with windows so darkly tinted she'd disappeared from view immediately. Sawyer hadn't left the petite blonde's side and Olivia had also been flanked almost immediately by a tall man with dark hair who seemed to be in charge.

"*Mon cher*, we'll be at the estate in just a few minutes. The staff has prepared dinner, we'll let them take care of our bags while we eat." When she started to protest, he pressed a finger against her lips, "We've given you space and a bit of time, love, but we will have dinner together and then we are going to talk." Carli wasn't sure she'd be able to explain what had happened, but it was clear she was going to face the music sooner than she'd hoped. She searched his eyes for any sign of anger or frustration, and found nothing but determination.

"Alright, but I'm not sure I have the answers you are

seeking."

"Shhh, we'll work it out, don't worry."

Parker turned and spoke over his shoulder as they passed through one of the most elaborate gates Carli had seen, "Princess, one of a Dom's responsibilities is to help the submissive in his care become all he or she can be. What that means to you is we'll push and prod until you'll probably want to run screaming into the night, but you'll always know we have your best interest at heart."

Swallowing hard, Carli tried to make sense out of his words. She wasn't fooled by his calm tone, there was steel at the core of both men's determination to find out what was going on in her head. Her problem was…she wasn't sure she could explain something she didn't fully understand herself. The driveway wound through trees and she did a double take when she saw a man standing at the edge of the trees—*what the hell?* The presence of that level of security reminded her why she was here and of the fact she hadn't checked in with her agency team. Pulling out her phone, she winced when she saw the number of missed calls, but it was Phillip's text message that caught her attention. His words were unusually harsh and his inquiry about her specific location didn't sound like him at all. Wondering what had happened to make him so angry, she started to reply but stopped. *What if he didn't send the message? What if someone is luring me out and simply using him to find out where I am?*

"Carli? What's wrong? You're white as a sheet." Tristan's voice brought her back to the moment and she realized he'd pulled the phone from her hand and then passed it to Parker.

"I started to answer and then realized that someone might be using him to find out where I am." Her voice sounded unsteady and that really frustrated her. She wasn't used to being in a position of weakness and she damned well didn't like it.

"Princess, I talked to Phillip before we left. I mentioned we might take you out of the city to spend a night or two in the country, and even though I didn't share our specific destination, your absence wouldn't be a surprise for him. He didn't sound upset when I spoke with him, would he have any reason to be angry with you?" Carli's first inclination was to be annoyed by Parker's insinuation, but when she thought about it, she realized he didn't understand their relationship, so it was a reasonable inquiry.

"No, I can't imagine why he'd be annoyed. We're friends and co-workers, but that's all."

"Does his income depend on you in any way?" Tristan had spoken softly, but the words still slammed into her chest like a cannon blast.

"Well, yes—I suppose so, at least to some degree. But he's very good at his job, so he'll just be assigned to another model when I retire and he's been advocating for Mallory to fill my position even though the owners of the agency are not sold on the idea. I'm not sure he is really that convinced she'd be capable of handling the pressure, but his current flame seems to be besties with her, so I think Phillip is humoring him." She hated to consider the implications of her own words, she wasn't sure she'd survive a betrayal of that magnitude. Phillip had been her only real friend during her time with the agency—*it simply has to be someone else.* They were interrupted when the SUV's door was pulled open by a man dressed in all black clothing reminiscent of that she'd seen on Special Forces soldiers when she'd done a photo shoot for a veteran's group. He was huge and the gun on his hip was more than a little bit intimidating.

"Go on, *mon cher,* he's part of my parents' security detail. The fact he is dressed like that tells you how seriously they are about seeing to your safety—ordinarily you'd never be able to pick out members of their security staff. My parents are quite insistent they look like guests, but you'll understand all that much better when you meet my mom and dad in a few days. To say they are a bit *casual* would be a tremendous understatement." Parker's snort of laughter and the smiles on the faces of those standing nearby made Carli curious—how casual could the couple be when they owned a home that looked more like a castle than a private residence? The place was ornate to the point of being borderline pretentious and from what she'd seen driving up, there were at least two large wings making her wonder what was sheltered in the back.

Carli's career had given her access to some of the most beautiful places in the world, but she'd always been whisked in and out so quickly she was rarely given the chance to truly appreciate the splendor or her surroundings, but stepping through the door of the Harris' home was something else altogether. No one pushed her quickly down a hall to a dressing room, they simply stood back and let her take it all in. Her breath caught at the marble floors as the lights gleamed off their polished surfaces. The gilded mirrors caught the indulgent expressions of the people waiting for her to move along, but Carli was too caught up in the moment to care that she'd essentially halted everyone's progress simply to enjoy the moment.

Matching curved staircases were the focal points of the entry with a chandelier hanging from the center that looked larger than most cars. "It's breathtaking, Tristan—I can't imagine what it must have been like growing up in a place like this." She hadn't been raised in poverty, but this far surpassed anything she'd ever seen in the home of someone she knew personally.

"It's lovely, but it can be overwhelming until you realize it's really just a home."

"A huge home filled with beautiful furnishings that someone spends a lot of time keeping in pristine condition. I've seen museums that weren't decorated this beautifully. Did your mom do the decorating? If so, she did an incredible job because it reflects a period of time when lavish elegance was supposed to be a class distinction, but this has all the beauty without making those who enter feel as though they don't belong. It's a home that someone cares enough about to hang family pictures that don't look like formal portraits painted by famous artists paid to make their subjects look regal and unattainable."

TRISTAN STARED AT Carli completely speechless, if he hadn't known better he'd have sworn he was listening to his mom describe the look she'd been striving for when she'd decorated the front hall. In that instant Tristan knew Carli was perfect for him, now he just needed to convince her. He'd seen Parker's growing certainty over the past few days, and it had solidified as soon as Carli had taken an emotional step back. Whether it was sincere knowledge that Carli was the woman they'd been waiting for or Parker's competitive nature, Tristan wasn't sure, but he knew his friend wasn't going to let her walk away until she'd explained her sudden change of heart.

Taking her small hand in his, Tristan led her down the hallway into the smaller of the two dining rooms. He'd been certain that's where Artem, his parents' longtime butler, would have set up their dinner and he wasn't disappointed. Giving the man a short nod of thanks, he was rewarded with a brief smile. For the first time he could remember, Artem looked fondly at a woman Tristan had brought to dinner that had to be some sort of a sign because the stuffy older man had been as cold as ice to every other woman Tristan had ever dated.

Their dinner was delicious and the wine perfect, but it was the woman sitting beside him that made the night special. She'd started to relax after the second glass of wine, but Parker had discretely set her glass aside when she'd nearly tipped over the fourth glass. After serving their dessert, the staff disappeared from view. Tristan knew Carli had noted their absence because she'd been trailing the tongs of her fork through the whipped cream on her strawberries in what looked like an elaborate Zen garden design. Her outward attempt to calm her mind made him want to take her in hand—he'd love to show her all the ways he and Parker could ease those turbulent thoughts.

"Princess, it's time for us to talk. Why don't you walk us through what happened during that scene? I'll remind you that you didn't use either of your safe words, so we're really swinging in the breeze here."

"*Mon cher*, you will never be punished for honesty as long as it is presented respectfully." Tristan watched her chew her lip in indecision, "Think of it like this, you were enjoying your introduction to the lifestyle up to that point, so it seems to me that you have a lot to gain by working it out, and even more to lose by letting your fear of transparency stand in your way."

He watched as she closed her eyes as if trying to pull strength from deep inside of herself, he wished she trusted them enough to let them take whatever burden she was carrying from her shoulders. Leaning back, Tristan watched Parker adopt a similarly casual pose as Carli fought an internal battle as she tried to sort through emotions he feared might be swamping her. "Let's try this, perhaps you can sort it through in your mind if you describe how you were feeling prior to the punishment scene."

Carli's eyes softened and she didn't even hesitate, "I felt cherished and protected. I don't remember a time when I felt as cared for—like you both really wanted me to be happy. Most people just want me to smile and look good—it's all about what the camera sees, no one cares enough to find out what's inside, you know?"

"Did you think we didn't care about you anymore, princess? That the punishment was a way to distance ourselves from you?" She didn't have to answer, the heartbreak moved across her face in living color. "Because, if that's the case, I want to clarify something—and I want it made crystal clear, you couldn't be more wrong. We used that punishment because spanking hadn't worked—quite frankly you've enjoyed the paddlings you've gotten so it's more of a reward than punishment. This was just an alternative—and obviously not a very good one. But unless you are honest with us, we have no way of knowing how wrong it's going. Had you used one of your safe words you could have saved us all a lot of trouble."

The first tear trailed down her porcelain cheek and Tristan had to resist the urge to pull her on to his lap and reassure her that everything would be alright. That wasn't what she needed, and wouldn't be helpful in the long run so he just waited. "I didn't realize I was in over my head until it was too late. My mind was caught up in your pleasure until the moment came when you pulled back and left me hanging…lost in my need." Her tears were a steady stream now and the urge to pull her close was almost overwhelming. "And then I got in the shower and everything fell apart."

What? Tristan had no idea she'd broken down immediately after the scene—that actually explained a lot. "*Mon cher*, explain what you mean when you say everything fell apart. Because it sounds like you are describing an adrenaline crash, something we should have watched for and absolutely something you should have mentioned." Tristan felt his chest tighten as she described how used she'd felt as she'd crouched alone and sobbing in the shower.

"Fuck." Parker's one word summed up Tristan's feelings perfectly.

Taking her hand in his, Tristan stood pulling her to her feet at the same time, "Come. Let's go for a walk. The gardens are beautiful in the moonlight." And seeing her bare skin bathed in the lunar glow would go a long way to bring him back to center. The cobblestone walkway was lined with tiny twinkling lights and the sound of falling water added to the ambience. His dad had spared no expense when his mother confessed to being homesick for her family's large Connecticut estate. She'd grown up with freedom afforded few of her social class, roaming the spacious gardens behind her family home had fed her free spirit and no doubt that time had a huge impact on the carefree adult she'd become.

Once they'd come to the first open space, Tristan turned to look down at Carli, her eyes were wide as she took in the small waterfall at the edge of the pool in front of them. "It's amazing. I'm not sure I've ever seen a pool like this one. The lights behind the waterfall and along the rock ledge make you believe you've come upon a secret garden in paradise. And the twinkling lights in the trees look like dancing fairies." He smiled down at her, God his mother was going to adore her, and his father would spoil her as shamelessly as he did his beautiful wife.

"Yes, it's lovely, but it pales in comparison to you, *mon cher*. There is only one problem, you're dressed and I want you naked. Master Parker and I want to reclaim what is ours. Strip for us, love." From the corner of his eye, Tristan saw Parker step forward from where he'd been standing in the shadows. Giving his friend a quick shake of his head, he waited as Carli seemed to process his sudden command. Under normal circumstances, a submissive's hesitation would have been an issue, but Tristan knew she hadn't actually been *hesitating,* rather she'd simply been catching up mentally. Since he'd been the one facing her, he'd seen how she'd been busy taking in her surroundings. She'd been lost in the moment and hadn't been ready for him to turn the tables on her so quickly.

As soon as she was completely bared to his view, Tristan stepped forward to draw his fingers down the top slopes of her breasts before tugging gently on her nipples. He knew they were probably still tender from being clamped earlier, so he deliberately teased gently and reveled in watching them draw up into even tighter peaks. God, he wanted to lay her out and devour every inch of her until her taste and scent surrounded him, but he and Parker needed to remind her why she'd agreed to try their lifestyle. Tristan wanted to replace the past several hours of discord between them with the soul-deep connection he knew had been just beyond their reach earlier. Once Carli understood the depth of commitment she'd experience in a ménage relationship, the easier it would be for them to solidify their places in her life.

Chapter Eighteen

Parker stepped in close behind Carli enjoying the warmth radiating from her naked skin. Encircling her wrists with his large hands, he simply let the feeling of being shackled wash over her for several seconds before sliding his hands slowly up her arms. Cupping the top of her biceps, he pulled her back against his chest leaning down to speak against her ear, "You take my breath away, princess. The moonlight loves you, it kisses your bare skin making you glow like the angel you are." Feeling her shudder under his touch sent a surge of blood to his cock threatening to short circuit his brain.

Tristan was smiling down at her and Parker enjoyed the fact he was currently in the enviable position of pressing his raging hard-on against her bare skin. He'd stripped while Tristan had been speaking to her and feeling his heated flesh pressing against the cooler smooth skin of her back pushed his control even closer to the edge. Parker could feel her skin heating against him, her soft moan let him know she was losing herself in the sensations, and that was exactly where they wanted her to be. Tristan stepped back and smiled down on her indulgently, "I'm going to watch you for a bit, *mon amōre*. I love seeing your eyes dilating as you fall further and further into the deep end of pleasure. We're going to show you just how much you'll enjoy giving yourself over into our care."

Parker wrapped his arms around her cupping both breasts, pinching her nipples just enough to elicit a soft gasp followed by the sweetest moan he'd ever heard. "That's it, princess, let go of all those troublesome little worries and just feel. Let yourself enjoy each touch, it will become more and more difficult for your body to tell the difference between pleasure and pain—and that means we're taking you exactly where we want you to go." Sliding one hand down over her flat abdomen, Parker's fingers found her slit and he smiled up at Tristan as he spoke to Carli, "You're so wet for us, princess—so perfectly responsive. The soft petals of your sex are flowering open as your sweet body prepares itself for us. Feeling your honey sliding over my fingers makes me want to push you up against the nearest tree and fuck you until you can't remember a time I wasn't buried deep inside you. Look at your other Master, sweetheart. Watch how his eyes take in everything from the dew misting your skin to the shift in your breathing. Did you know those soft panting breathes are a siren's call to a Dom? And watching your pulse pick up as it pounds against the base of your throat tells us your body will soon be glowing as it flushes a glorious rose. All of those signs tell a Dom how much you are enjoying his touch." He wouldn't tell her yet, but watching was one of the many reasons they loved sharing, she'd learn soon enough how much they would enjoy sitting back to watch as the other played.

"It is important for you to remember, that while we are indeed very well trained in reading body language, that doesn't mean we won't make mistakes—particularly until we get to know you better." Tristan was watching her so closely Parker doubted he'd miss anything, but the message was still one she needed to hear.

"Eventually we'll know you better than you know yourself, princess—but that will take time." Parker could feel her pressing back closer as they talked and while he loved her responsiveness, he was concerned their words might be falling on deaf ears.

"Until we have had time to establish the bond needed to know all we need to know, we need to know you are communicating with us. I think it's safe to say we would all like to avoid repeating the mistakes that were made on the flight here." Parker knew his friend had deliberately understated the problem that had nearly torn her from their arms, but agreed there was little to be gained by rehashing it.

Parker was sliding his long middle finger in and out of her channel. Carli's pussy was drenched with her cream and even though he knew many women were embarrassed by the sounds made by all that wonderful moisture, personally he found it a complete turn on. "Feeling your sweet pussy sucking on my fingers, hearing those hungry sounds—God, baby, that makes me crazy." Tristan moved to stand in front of her after stripping out of his clothing, he pulled long strokes on his cock as his gaze centered on the junction of her thighs, he watched Parker's fingers moving in and out of her bare sex.

"I love that your pubis is smooth as silk, *mon cher*. Fuck, those treatments are worth their weight in gold. I know you said you had started treatments again, and I promise we're going to let you finish them. We'll love having your backdoor permanently denuded as well, but one of us will accompany you to each of those appointments."

At her soft gasp of surprise, Parker chuckled, "That's right, princess, no one—and I do mean no one touches this luscious ass without one of us there. This point is non-negotiable. Part of our job is to protect you, frankly between you, your sister, and now my own sister—I'm starting to think protecting the three of you is going to be a full-time job." He really wished he had listened to his business partners and brought on more staff before they'd left. Parker had been off his game for the past several months—feeling disconnected from everything around him. But the fog had started clearing from his mind as soon as Carli was between the two of them. Shaking off his introspection, all he could do was hope like hell Tristan didn't notice the difference—Tristan's interminable psychoanalysis would drive Parker insane.

Drawing small circles around her clit with his fingers, Parker was pleased the shy little bundle of nerves had already emerged from hiding—it was seeking his attention and he didn't intend to disappoint. They'd discovered several *hot spots* on their responsive sub, but this one was purely magical. When instinct took over and Carli's hips began bucking wildly against him, Parker pinched the pink pleasure button, then letting his words waft over her ear, he rasped, "Come for us, princess."

There hadn't been more than a heartbeat between his command and Carli's release, she'd gone over before the words had settled in the air. God, he loved the sounds she made when she came and seeing the expression on Tristan's face told him his friend was right there with him. Aftershocks moved through her slender frame before she sagged in his arms. Sweetly spent and sex-limp Parker didn't let go of her fearing she'd slide to the floor and curl up like a sleepy kitten.

Tristan stepped forward pulling her into his embrace, "*Mon cher*, I'll never tire of watching you take your pleasure. Seeing you respond so perfectly fills a place in my heart I didn't even know existed." They quickly settled her over one of the lush garden's hidden features, Parker loved the way she roused when he stroked his hand down her spine.

Tristan had helped his dad rebuild the gardens a couple of years earlier, and the elder Harris was thrilled with the kinky surprises his son had incorporated. Leaning down he pressed a scorching kiss to Carli's lips, and Parker would bet his friend was spearing his tongue deep, plundering her mouth with the same ferocity he planned to use when he pushed his cock deep into her pussy. The move seemed to reawaken her body and from his position behind her, Parker saw moisture beading atop the swollen pink folds of her sex—damn he loved the way she looked spread out before him like a juicy feast.

Pressing deep into her heat as he watched his best friend move quickly so he could push himself between her ruby lips, watching them while her heat surrounded him threatened Parker's control—something that had rarely happened before Carli. Pushing everything from his mind except the pleasure coursing through him, Parker let go and lost himself in her sweet body. Tristan matched his demanding pace, keeping in time so they filled her from both ends in alternating, quick strokes. When Parker felt her vaginal muscles begin to quiver, he growled, "Come with us, princess."

All three of them let go at exactly the same moment and for the first time in his life Parker wondered if he would pass out from the pleasure. Brilliant bursts of color exploded behind his closed eyes in a display that shamed New York's Fourth of July celebrations. By the time he had emptied himself in her he didn't trust his legs to hold him upright, he leaned over her gasping and silently cursing how easily she swept him up in her passion. Tristan had dropped to his knees in front of her and Parker could hear his tender words telling Carli how perfect she was for the two of them. *Hell, it's a good thing one of us can still talk.*

Over the roaring in his ears, he heard Carli say she thought their jet was a time travel machine because she was certain the Knights had just introduced her to their jousting sticks. Tristan's head fell back as he laughed and Parker couldn't hold back his own chuckle at her quick wit. "I don't know, Master Tristan, but I think we might not have done our job if our beautiful sub is able to think so quickly—hell, I'm barely managing to stay conscious." He gave her a quick swat with the flat of his hand making her squeak in surprise.

By the time they cleaned up and made their way back to the master suite in Tristan's wing, Carli was fast asleep in his arms. Tucking her into bed, then looking down on her, he shook his head, "You know, she has one of the most recognizable faces in the world—but we're the only ones who get to see her like this. Maybe I'm really arrogant, but I find that knowledge tremendously satisfying."

"Well, you're not alone in that arrogance, brother. There is a depth to her beauty that the camera eludes to, but can't quite capture it. It's the essence of who she is at her core and there is a large part of me that is very grateful only those closest to her are allowed to glimpse it." Tristan was leaning against one of the thick walnut bedposts looking down with hooded eyes as Carli lay sleeping peacefully in his bed. Parker hadn't thought about how she would look in his own bed at his parents' Houston estate until this moment—and now he knew the thought would haunt him until he had the chance to take her *home*.

LAWTON HAD BEEN staring at the bank of monitors in the security office at The Knight's Club for hours trying to catch the intruder they expected to make an appearance. The anonymous tip he'd received had been bounced all around the world. He'd finally traced it back far enough to discover it had originated on a computer assigned to the modeling agency Carli Walker worked for, but that was as far back as Lawton had gotten before the club opened and he was fairly certain he'd been led there on purpose. They'd deliberately "leaked" the news his new wife and her sister would be visiting the club this weekend, but he was more than a little surprised things had developed so quickly.

Running his hand through his hair, Lawton leaned back in his chair and used the joystick to pan the outside cameras looking for any sign of uninvited guests. He was glad Tristan had insisted they install both regular and night vision cameras because the entire property was visible in amazing detail. Glancing back at the inside feeds, he smiled when Brodie shook his head no when Cressida waved her empty glass at him. She clearly wanted another glass of wine and frowned when the bartender slid a bottle of water in front of her. *Oh, baby, that frown is going to cost you dearly later.*

When he turned back to check the outside of the building he saw a small figure dressed entirely in black trying to open the door leading to their liquor storage area. Pulling the radio close, he updated the rest of the team, "Heads up, boys and girls, we have someone trying to access the backdoor behind the bar. Dressed all in black, approach with caution, I don't see a weapon, but that certainly doesn't mean he or she isn't armed." Before he'd even finished speaking, Brodie was practically dragging Cressida out of the area, she'd be locked in Tristan's office while they interviewed the intruder in a smaller, much more sterile space across the hall.

Lawton looked on as one of their employees moved in behind the dark clothed figure but before he could secure the perpetrator, there was an explosion of activity and in a few seconds their man was lying unmoving on the ground and their intruder was sprinting down the dark alley. Law sighed and leaned back in his chair. There was no way anyone was going to catch him now, and their first obligation was to check on their teammate who was being swarmed by people. Lawton was relieved to see them helping him to his feet, and anxious to find out what had happened.

An hour later Lawton leaned against the stone fireplace mantle in Tristan's office and swirled the last bit of whiskey around in the bottom of his glass. "Well, that didn't work out well."

"What? That we've now blown our one and only plan to find out who was behind the attack on our wife or the embarrassing fact that our man got his ass handed to him despite the fact he was at least a half foot taller and fifty pounds heavier than his opponent? Parker needs a more aggressive training program." Lawton could hear the frustration in Brodie's voice, but knew he wasn't actually angry.

"I agree, but let's face it, until Cressida and Carli entered our lives it wasn't really an issue."

"True enough—but just look at her, she looks like a sleeping angel not a trouble magnet. How could anyone want to hurt her? She represents everything that is good and right in the world." Brodie stood at the end of the sofa where Cressida lay curled up fast asleep, her hair fanned out over a golden pillow making it look like she had a halo, just like the angel he'd likened her to.

"Don't forget, she was just convenient—a way to send a message to Carli. I don't think either of them have ever made a secret of the fact they are close, so Cressida was an easy way to hurt Carli even without having access to her." Lawton would never forget the horror of watching Cressida fall down those stairs—the helplessness had been gut wrenching.

Brodie leaned down to push a strand of hair back behind Cressida's ear, "We've been given a second chance with her—it could have ended so differently. I thank God a hundred times a day that she wasn't taken from us."

"The man who engaged our would-be intruder said the guy had to have been trained in martial arts." Evan Williams had been working for Parker since leaving the Navy a year ago, so he was certainly in good enough physical condition.

"Evan said he recognized some of the moves as Krav Maga, so I'm contacting the local training centers to see if they have any members who match the description Evan gave us." Lawton didn't hold out much hope of tracking down any leads because from what he'd heard the centers were all small, the community was close-knit, and they tended to protect their own—much like the BDSM community. "I sent a message to Parker, but with the time difference, I doubt we'll hear from him for a few hours. I also sent the video of the encounter, just in case anything about the man seems familiar to Carli." Lawton watched Cressida shift restlessly, he noted she didn't sleep soundly unless either he or Brodie was lying close enough for her to touch.

"Did you remember to note Evan's comment about the man's accent?" Lawton smiled and nodded, he had remembered because it wasn't every day that you encountered someone who could curse at you with a Scottish lilt in their voice. If anything was going to help him with the Krav Maga training centers it would be the accent, but it was still a long shot.

"Let's get our wife home. She is still recovering and I hated exposing her to all of this tonight. But to be perfectly honest, I didn't want to fight with her either and she really does deserve the chance to see this thing through. To her credit, she came up here without any argument when I heard your call, and I know she needs to feel like she's helping." Brodie pulled his phone out and called for their car to be brought around to the front before pulling the soft subbie blanket around Cressida as Lawton secured the room. "The dark circles under her eyes give away her exhaustion even though she insists she's fine."

"I am fine—really. But watching all of the scenes downstairs made me horny. I want you—both of you." Cressida's sleepy voice went straight to Lawton's cock, and despite knowing how important it was for her to rest, his dick had other plans. "Please...if I promise to sleep in tomorrow?" When neither of them answered as they walked out the club's front door, he heard her sigh, "I'm getting sex tonight if I have to dance on the table naked like that girl whose Master was pretending to play poker all night."

Brodie leaned down to place her in Lawton's waiting arms before seating himself in the back of the car, "Pet, did you also notice the strapping she got for that attention seeking stunt?"

"Yes, and I'd happily skip that part in the interest of conserving time and energy. We can skip right on to the screaming orgasm part...you know, like the one she got afterward." Brodie was grinning as he sat next to them, good Lord she was quick.

Lawton tightened his hold on the woman who held his heart in her small hands. "This is one of those moments when your Doms have to decide if what you want and what is best for you are the same." When she tipped her face up to his, the pleading look in her eyes did him in—and the decision was made in that instant. "We'll make love to you, sweet wife, but you'll sleep an extra hour and skip your morning workout tomorrow. You've had a long day and we don't want you to push yourself." She leaned up and kissed his chin before burrowing close. Had he given in too easily? Probably. Did he care that he should probably have his Dom card shredded and the pieces burned on a sacrificial alter for letting her top from the bottom? Not in the least.

Chapter Nineteen

CARLI LISTENED INTENTLY as Parker outlined what had happened outside The Knight's Club the night before—she still couldn't believe she'd slept almost fourteen hours straight. Nothing about the man in the video had seemed familiar, but at Parker's mention of the Scottish accent she stiffened. "Wait, Phillip's latest squeeze is from Scotland, although I think he's lived in the United States for a long time. I've only met him a few times, honestly I don't make much effort to befriend the men who parade through Phillip's bedroom, but I did notice he and Mallory seemed to be particularly close. I didn't care enough to pay attention—I don't even know his name, but they did spend a lot of time huddled together talking—I just assumed they both had agendas with Phillip and they were using one another to get what they wanted."

Parker was already dialing his phone before she'd stopped speaking, and when she looked to Tristan, he was shaking his head, *"Mon cher*, do you think it's possible you have underestimated Phillip's interest in you?" She was genuinely confused by his question since she'd already explained that her friend was gay. "Is it possible Phillip is actually bi-sexual? That would go a long way to explain why his current lover was attempting to break into a private club where he thought he would find you."

It was just too much to think about, even with all the sleep she'd had, she would still have to fight jet lag for several more days before her body became accustomed to the new schedule. The one part of traveling she'd never managed to overcome, and one of the things she'd miss the least when she cut back in the coming months. Standing, she asked, "Do you mind if I go for a swim before dinner? I need to do something to wake up my muscles and brain—I'm too sluggish to think clearly."

"Please make yourself at home, love. You are welcome to use any of the facilities at any time." She must have looked surprised when he stood because he grinned, "Since we aren't sure who we are dealing with, and I'd prefer the members of our security staff don't see you naked, I'll go with you. Parker and I are actually quite possessive about what we consider ours." *Naked? She didn't plan to swim naked.* He laughed and kissed her before she had a chance to speak, "Yes, you will swim naked, because I want to enjoy the view and you are already wearing far more than I'd prefer."

He'd wrapped his hand around her wrist and pulled her along as he made his way out the back of the house. Tristan stopped to speak with one of the staff, and even though Carli spoke French, she certainly didn't speak it as fluently as Tristan, who had spoken so quickly to the man standing at the back door she'd barely caught anything aside from a quick warning to keep everyone away from the pool area. She could only hope the rest of the conversation had included a request to shut down the security cameras in that area—she had no desire to see her bare ass on YouTube.

When they reached the pool area, Carli once again took a long look around the lushly landscaped area, but this time she noted the high walls hidden behind the hedge and foliage along both ends. Tristan had obviously followed her line of sight because when she returned her attention to him, he was smiling down at her. "You're so very observant, *mon amour*. There is a retractable dome for this area during the winter, I suspect Dad will put it up before their trip to the islands later this month. It's much like those of the larger stadiums in the United States, it's quite fun to watch slide into place actually. But right now I'd much prefer to watch you swim. Strip, love."

This time Carli kept up with Tristan's quick change of direction in the conversation and she was out of her clothing in record time. "You are stunning, *mon cher*." She trembled when he ran his fingers down her cheek trailing the pads along her jaw until he could wrap his large palm around the side of her neck. The move focused her attention on him, letting all the concerns clouding her mind fall away—the peace in that moment helped her understand submission's appeal for her younger sister. "You are beginning to understand, aren't you, love? I see it in your eyes. Think about how wonderful it would be to be able to push all those troubling thoughts and uncertainties out of your mind and let your Masters shelter you. We aren't twenty-four/seven Doms, Carli. We don't want to run your life, though we are both probably more possessive than any men you have previously dated. The one thing we'll never negotiate on is your safety."

Carli nodded in understanding, she'd heard Cressi say the same thing about her husbands and at least in theory, Carli agreed—although things might look far different in practice. It probably didn't matter, since they would likely have already moved on before that became an issue anyway. One of the things Carli had learned early in her career was that men were in love with the *idea* of dating a model—the *reality* of it was far less appealing. It wasn't the glamorous lifestyle everyone assumed it was—not by a long shot.

"Swim, love. When you're finished, we'll discuss our schedule for the next few days." Carli knew she'd surprised Tristan when she'd leaned forward and wrapped her arms around him hugging him tightly, because it was the first time she'd initiated physical intimacy between them. *"Mon cher?"* It really wasn't fair that she'd held them at arm's length, they'd been incredibly patient with her, and it was time to do more than *take*. She didn't answer, Carli just smiled sweetly at him before turning and diving smoothly into the crystal blue water.

TRISTAN LEANED BACK against the leather seat as the helicopter lifted off the helipad enjoying the sea of lights spread out below them as they skimmed over London's beautiful skyline. He'd always loved seeing the city awash in twinkling lights—somehow it seemed cleaner, fresher at night. They'd enjoyed dinner at one of the city's most exclusive restaurants, the food had been a feast for both the eyes and the palate, but that hadn't been why they'd chosen it. *Whipped* was owned by one of London's most prominent Masters, he also owned and operated the club occupying the lower levels of the building. Even though annual club membership fees started at six figures, many of the members had no idea the restaurant even existed.

Carli hadn't voiced her concerns when they'd dressed her, but she hadn't been able to hide her frown when Parker informed her the short midnight blue dress and strappy sandals were indeed all they intended for her to wear. As they'd stepped up to the maître d' stand, Parker had taken the lead while Tristan slipped his hand beneath her short dress, "Spread those pretty legs for me, love, I have a surprise for you." Her soft gasp of surprise made him smile, "*Mon cher*, this is a very special establishment. Do you trust us to keep you safe?" She nodded without hesitation and quickly moved her legs far enough apart he could easily slide his fingers through the soft folds of her sex. "So wet—so perfect." As he continued speaking, he rolled the small egg along the length of her pussy coating it with her slick honey. "You may see things this evening that surprise you. What are your safe words, Carli?" When she'd recited them to him, Tristan leaned down to bite down gently on the tender spot where her neck and shoulders met. "Most of the other patrons will be observing higher protocol than we will expect from you, but I want to be sure you understand what we'll expect."

Parker turned to kiss her forehead, "Princess, it's very important that you remember you are only allowed to speak to your own Masters or to speak to others when we give you specific permission to do so. You'll have few opportunities to speak to anyone else, so it shouldn't be an issue."

Tristan slipped the small egg deep into her channel and smiled at her soft moan of need when he withdrew his fingers. "You're lovely and seeing the rosy flush of arousal spread over your chest tempts me in ways I can't even tell you." He loved how the dress they'd chosen for her draped precariously low in both the front and the back baring so much of her skin to their touch. The fabric skimmed over her soft skin and did nothing to hide the tight points of her nipples, and the dark color emphasized her ivory perfection and the lovely flush of arousal spreading quickly over her chest.

"Agreed. If we get through this meal without fucking her on the table it's going to be a small miracle." Parker's crude words broke the spell they'd all fallen under and Tristan suspected that had been his friend's intent. Thankfully their table was ready and they quickly settled in. Their food had been served immediately, both Parker and Tristan chuckled at the surprised look on Carli's face.

"The owner is a Master, princess, he understands how tempting little subs can be, so he requires orders be placed when the reservations are made. As a matter of fact, I believe one of his favorite pets is celebrating a birthday today, so we'll get to watch his birthday spanking." Tristan noticed his friend hadn't mentioned everyone in the restaurant would be invited to administer a couple of swats. Last year the man had sported the telltale bruises of a well-punished sub for weeks, but the successful London barrister had sworn it had been the best birthday gift he'd ever received.

"Master Leland trains both Doms and subs, *mon cher*— he frequently has them perform here. Keep in mind everything you see is consensual, but if you see something that bothers you we want you to let us know immediately." Tristan would like to avoid any of the hard-core punishment scenes he'd seen played out on the restaurant's small stage simply because he didn't feel Carli was ready to see anything that intense. Neither he nor Parker were sadists and watching those scenes didn't do anything for either of them.

"Enough about Master Leland, I'm much more interested in you, princess. Did Master Tristan give you our gift?" He and Parker both had small remotes in their pockets, and Carli's soft gasp let him know his friend had switched on the miniature egg vibrator. "That sweet sound goes straight to my cock, baby." They'd made her come twice during dinner which explained why she was sleeping soundly in the seat next to him now.

The messages they'd received from Lawton cut their dinner short, knowing Carli's co-workers were in London had shaken her and they'd wanted to get her back to the estate as quickly as possible. As an added precaution, Tristan had contacted his parents requesting they return to the estate immediately as well. Their downtown penthouse had a state of the art security system, but there wasn't any question the country estate offered the best opportunity to keep his mother out of the line of fire.

Tristan loved his mother, but her insistence that everyone was good at their core made her a security nightmare. He'd listened in as James Mikels tried unsuccessfully to convince Mary Elizabeth Harris allowing a member of her security detail inside the boutiques while she shopped was crucial to their ability to keep her safe. Her response had been simple, "Hogwash. The men you hire are big and scary, they frighten women and small children, James." As a compromise, his mother had agreed to learn how to shoot and to carry a small weapon anytime she would be out of her bodyguard's line of sight or there would be walls between them on her frequent shopping sprees. Of course, the last he'd heard, she was still refusing to carry ammunition and consequently, James was still pulling his hair out in frustration.

Tristan hated the fact Carli had a photo shoot in a few days, protecting her in so many different locations around the city was a logistical nightmare, particularly when the danger appeared to be from those with the most access.

Once they'd settled Carli in bed, Tristan planned to speak with Parker about hiring a different photo-team to take the shots her agency had promised the tourism board, he doubted her agency would be on board, but worth a try.

Chapter Twenty

CARLI WOKE UP alone in the enormous bed and wondered once again how she'd managed to sleep so long. Cressi had insisted orgasms were better than any sleeping aid ever invented—Carli laughed at her younger sister's exaggeration, but she was going to have to revisit and revise her opinion as her father used to say. Stretching, she thought back over their dinner the evening before—everything had been exciting and perfect until the maître d' pulled both men aside to check their phones. Carli appreciated the fact the restaurant didn't allow any electronic devices past the front entrance, knowing she wouldn't see her picture plastered all over the internet had allowed her to freely enjoy the pleasure they'd given her during dinner.

Once she'd learned her co-workers were in London, she had completely lost all focus and was relieved when they'd quickly exited the restaurant and flown back to the estate. Perhaps her sense of security here was unfounded, but she'd been able to relax once she'd known they were safely on their way back to the Harris' country home. She vaguely remembered Tristan tucking her into bed—*did he say his parents would be here today or did I dream that?*

Making her way into the large master bedroom's en suite, she noticed they'd laid out clothes for her to wear and laughed to herself—*I guess that answers my question.*

There was a large bouquet of wildflowers sitting on a table, Carli stopped to enjoy the various blooms and smiled. Knowing they'd remembered her casual remark that first night showed her they'd been listening, no one had ever sent her wildflowers, Carli picked up the small card and read: *To our beautiful damsel, here's to wild nights with grateful Knights and riding off under the stars on a silver steed.*

Carli wanted to laugh and cry at the same time—last night had been wild indeed and before she'd fallen asleep, she'd thanked them for the special night and letting her skim the stars on their silver steed. Their special gesture filled her heart with joy and she couldn't wait to get downstairs and thank them. She was cleaned up and downstairs in less than an hour, but she was surprised to find the kitchen bustling with people.

Seeing so many people she didn't recognize stopped her in her tracks. There was a distinguished looking man who appeared to be looking over schematics with James Mikels and several other men who looked like they'd be more comfortable on a battlefield than in the kitchen belonging to a member of Great Britain's aristocracy. As soon as the man standing beside James looked up, Carli knew she was looking at Tristan's father—the resemblance was unmistakable.

William Harris' face lit up with a smile and he quickly made his way over to her, "Good morning, sweetheart. I'm William Harris, Tristan's father." He pulled her into a hug and she couldn't help but smile, Tristan hadn't been kidding about his parents being far from what she'd expected. A high-pitched squeal from the other side of the room startled her, and William pulled back kissing her on the forehead, "We'll get to know one another later, my wife is about to steamroll us and steal you away."

He'd been right as a slender woman about Carli's height yanked her from William's grasp and enfolded her in a tight hug. "I'm so happy to finally meet you. My son threatened to toss me into the sea if I woke you and my loving husband hasn't let me out of his sight. I'm baffled by their lack of faith in me."

Carli heard William's soft laughter, "Darling, we know you all too well. You are like a kid at Christmas—no patience whatsoever."

Before Carli realized what was happening, she was seated at the breakfast bar as Mary Elizabeth Harris slid several plates filled with various breakfast selections in front of her. "I wasn't sure what you would like, so I made a bit of everything." Carli's confusion must have shown, because Tristan's mom laughed, "Oh, dear—don't worry, the men will eat anything you push to the side. I've been putting them off for an hour and you'd think they hadn't eaten in weeks. The cooks don't much like me taking over their kitchen, but occasionally I get the urge to make a nice American breakfast."

Tristan slid gracefully on to the chair next to her and leaned over to kiss her on the cheek. "Good morning, *mon cher*. I see you've already been besieged by my mother. I hope you were properly introduced." She could only blink at him in overwhelmed surprise—talk about feeling like you'd been dropped into the middle of the deep end. He quickly made introductions around the room and Carli tried desperately to commit all of the names to memory. "Don't worry about the names, you'll get them. They are here to protect you—typically I believe in treating staff as family, but in your case I'm making an exception so they are all on point for the foreseeable future."

Carli leaned close, speaking softly, "Thank you for the

lovely flowers—you'll spoil me."

"*Mon amour,* you are most welcome. And spoiling you is my life's goal." His hand wrapped around the side of her neck, his thumb stroking slowly over the pounding pulse at the base of her throat.

"Tristan, dear, have you given Carli a weapon? She and I could go to the range after breakfast. I haven't been there in a while, and it would give us something to do while you and the other boys try to figure out how to take over the world. I swear Dwight Eisenhower planned the invasion of Normandy with less fanfare." Carli giggled, she'd forgotten that Tristan's mother was American, which explained her familiarity with the U.S. General who'd spearheaded one of the largest military operations in history.

Once Carli convinced Tristan she'd eaten all the breakfast she possibly could, he'd reluctantly agreed to let her walk down to the shooting range with his mom. He'd gotten her a small Ruger from the large gun safe in his father's office and reviewed its operation in excruciating detail until she wanted to slap him. She'd finally grasped his hand with her own, "Tristan, I used a gun just like this one when I learned to shoot." When she'd first moved to New York she'd been so terrified by all the stories she'd heard, she'd taken lessons at a range not far from her apartment. She'd gotten her permit, but had never gotten around to actually purchasing a gun of her own.

When Tristan and Parker balked at the women walking the short distance alone, Mary Elizabeth had finally had enough. "Listen to me you two Neanderthals. The range is less than a hundred yards and you know perfectly well there are enough cameras between here and there you'll be able to see every breath she takes. Damn, boys, you are going to smother her if you don't lighten up." Then turning to her husband, her tone changed so dramatically Carli almost laughed out loud. "William, darling, you're always the voice of reason. Be our knight in shining armor and make the boys stop picking on their girl."

"You are my soul and my heart's inspiration, but you are incorrigible." William laughed and kissed her on the tip of her nose.

"Aww, The Righteous Brothers—one of my favorites. You are such a romantic devil...handsome, too."

Carli hadn't realized she was staring until she felt Tristan's fingers smoothing down her cheek. "I've always dreamed of having a relationship like theirs. Parker's parents act the same way—that's what we're hoping to build with you, *mon cher*." Carli knew her surprise must have shown because he chuckled, "You didn't think we were just playing, did you, love? Because I assure you that is not the case. Now, go down to the range, Parker or I will be along in a few minutes to see how you are doing."

Parker walked around the table to kiss her—*Good Lord, you'd think I was leaving the country instead of just walking across the yard.* "Olivia is swimming and Sawyer is standing by in that area, just so you know. We'll let him know you're headed their way so be sure he sees you."

Mary Elizabeth rolled her eyes, "Oh for heaven's sake. Perhaps we should just take walkie-talkies so we could check in every few feet. This is getting out of hand."

William leaned over swatting his lovely wife, "Baby, we'll be chatting more about this later, but for now, be careful. Carli belongs to the boys so you'll need to respect that—just as I expect them to respect that you belong to me." *Well, well. Isn't that interesting?* Evidently Tristan had inherited more than just his handsome face from his father.

Making their way through the beautiful gardens, Mary

Elizabeth chatted about the flowers that were currently blooming in brilliant shades of red and yellow all around them, and the details her extensive plans to enhance the landscaping next spring. As they neared the pool area Carli heard Olivia Daniels voice fill the air, "You know what, Sawyer? I'm half a heartbeat away from shoving your starchy ass in the pool." The low murmur of a man's voice rumbled just before a loud splash. Then Olivia's sputtering voice once again sounded, "You are an ass. I ought to just shoot you with your own gun."

Carli giggled when she realized both she and Mary Elizabeth had stopped and were peeking through the thick shrubbery watching the scene play out in front of them. "Imp, we have an audience, so you'd have witnesses. Swim your laps so I can get you back into the house where I know you can't cause trouble—well, not as much trouble anyway. What the hell were you trying to do in the kitchen anyway, blow up Britain? For a scientist you don't seem to be able to read a recipe worth a damn."

This time Olivia's voice had the distinctive quiver of a woman reaching the end of her rope, "I was hungry, I wanted pancakes—and contrary to what your bestie thinks, I did not make them as a prototype for Goodyear. That observation was just mean." Carli watched as Olivia pushed off from the side and began swimming in perfectly measured strokes down the length of the pool before executing a seamless underwater turn then resuming her exercise.

Sawyer's expression went from stern to regretful for just a few seconds before he turned his attention to them. "Ladies, I'll let your men know you've checked in. Good luck at the range." He returned his attention to the slender woman pounding the water with such force Carli wonder if she was taking out her frustrations on the water or herself. Carli could relate.

OLIVIA WAS SO damned mad she worried she might actually drown by the time she finished her swim. James Mikels and Sawyer Hughes had to be the most annoying men on the planet—hell, they'd even knocked her older brother to third place. *You don't want to jump your brother's bones, that's why he's in frick-fracking third place.* In Olivia's opinion, if the government really wanted world peace they should mandate a daily requirement for orgasms—like vitamins and minerals. Those happy brain chemicals had a better chance of maintaining peace than the nuclear weapons they paid her to track. And a couple of 'scream-the-walls-down' releases might actually keep her from strangling the two men who had become her self-appointed wardens.

She shouldn't have threatened to shoot him—she knew that was inappropriate, as well as freaking impossible, he'd probably tie her up like a pretzel and set her on the mantle in James's sitting room. *Cripes, who has a damned sitting room, anyway? Pretentious bastard.* As she neared the side of the pool and prepared to turn, she was yanked roughly from the water by a slender man dressed all in black. "Whoa, what the hell? Who are you?"

His eyes were wide as he looked her over in distaste, she knew immediately he wasn't there for her because there hadn't been even a spark of recognition in his wide, dilated eyes. He reminded her of some of the homeless drug addicts she often saw begging outside the train station. She sensed the man's desperation and recognized the seriousness of the situation—her brother had always warned her that there was a fine line between fear and desperation...and either one made people unpredictable and dangerous. Glancing around, he spotted Sawyer laying on the concrete apron of the swimming pool, blood pooling beneath his head. Waving his gun in front of her face to get her attention, the man holding her arm practically snarled at her, "Don't worry about him, he isn't going to help you. Take me to Carli Walker—*now*."

"Carli? I don't know where she is. I haven't talked to her in days." *Well, at least part of that was true.* Olivia had heard Sawyer's end of the conversation earlier and knew the women were going to the gun range, but she wasn't sure which building on the enormous compound held that particular amenity. The Harris' estate was like a five star resort for adults. The waterfall and pool area, elaborate gardens, fishing pond, gym—the list went on and on.

He extended his arm, pointing the gun he held in Sawyer's direction, "You're a terrible liar, bitch. Take me to her or I'll finish what I started over there—quite frankly it's all the same to me." When she started to reach for her towel, he yanked her arm hard enough to make her yelp. "No—perhaps if you are cold you'll be more motivated to find Miss Perfect. The sooner we get this done, the sooner I'll have my lover all to myself." *Okay, now I know he's delusional, too, because nobody could love this asshat.*

She walked slowly toward the building she thought was her best bet. Olivia knew the longer she took to find Carli the greater their chances of being seen on the surveillance system. Since he hadn't let her slip on her shoes, it was easy to pick her way carefully along the cobblestone walkway—damn those rocks were really pretty, but they were hell on the bottoms of her tender feet. When he gave her arm a sharp tug, she yelled, "Stop it, this is your own fault, you should have let me wear shoes. Take off your own shoes and see how tough you are on these damned rocks, jerk."

"Perhaps I would have let you wear them if they hadn't been butt-fucking-ugly. Jesus, woman, have you no sense of fashion at all?" *Great, I've been kidnapped by a fashion snob.* And didn't it just figure—she'd always been the small, geeky-girl with parents who both always looked like they were headed to a photo session or a red carpet, and a brother who was the definition of hunk according to her friends. Yeah, it was great fun for a science nerd to grow up in Daniels family—*Not!*

Reminding herself to keep talking, Olivia asked, "Why do you want to talk to Carli? Is she a friend of yours?" *Brilliant, Olivia—everybody shows up with a gun, knocks out a guy twice his size, and kidnaps a dripping wet woman to escort around an estate when he's looking for his best friend.* He shot her a look usually reserved for insect infestations and simply rolled his eyes. "Hey, you could at least talk to me after insulting my shoes. It's not like you're making a rip-roaring fashion statement there, Mr. Monochromatic I-want-to-be-a-Ninja-when-I-grow-up. So, I'm sort of wondering what your connection is to one of the world's most successful supermodels."

His grip on her upper arm tightened to the point she knew she'd have a bruise there tomorrow—if she managed to live that long. "Good God. Are you always this annoying?" He gave her arm a yank almost sending her to her knees. "Carli Walker is the only thing standing between me and everything I want. My lover is in love with the ungrateful bitch and he won't accept the fact she doesn't see him that way. Mal and I are all he needs, but he isn't going to let go of that illusion until she's gone. And I plan to arrange it. Spending eternity in a nice dark box ought to work out perfectly for her—I hear she has a real fear of that sort of thing." His laugh made Olivia think of all the maniacal crazies she'd seen in the movies…*that's probably more accurate than you know, Liv.* Great, now she was talking to herself, perfect, she was going to die after being exposed to contagious insanity.

Olivia knew they were very close to the long building she assumed held the shooting range and she'd run out of ways to stall. They walked the length of the building without hearing any gunfire, so she hoped the women had already moved back to the house. When she glanced up at the camera, he rolled his eyes and laughed. "Give it up. Your knights aren't going to ride in on their white horses brandishing their silver swords and slay the dragon for you, lady. Mal has them all distracted and everything looks perfectly normal in their monitors." Her heart sank when she realized she was on her own—even though she wasn't his intended target, Olivia knew he'd never leave her alive.

As they rounded the corner of the building, the sound of a snapping twig made her pause just long enough for the man following her to crash into her back. The impact was enough to send her sprawling face first onto the rock path as the world around her erupted in chaos and an explosion of pain in her shoulder made her see stars a split second before the world went dark.

Chapter Twenty-One

JAMES MIKELS SMILED as he watched Olivia swim laps in the Harris' pool. Even in the monitor he could see the muscles in her shoulders flexing with each stroke. The extra effort she was putting into the movements told him she was becoming as sexually frustrated as he was. But he and Sawyer agreed that until they were certain she fully understood what she'd be getting into, they'd keep sex out of the mix. The few seconds he'd taken to confirm she was still safely tucked away in the center of the estate was a welcome respite from the pandemonium that had erupted minutes ago. The crazy woman who had managed to crash through the front gates had abandoned her disabled automobile and was now distracting most of his security team—how she'd continued to elude capture was something they'd be addressing in short order. However, first they needed to drop a net over her.

He'd been listening to the radio traffic when one of his men asked for confirmation Carli Walker was indeed still accounted for, explaining the woman they were chasing resembled their famous guest. Parker and Tristan had both cursed at that information as they'd run out the front door to help. If this was the woman who had hurt Carli's sister, James wondered what condition she'd be in when they turned her over to the local authorities.

Without taking his eyes off Olivia, James hit the speed dial on his phone for Sawyer. He didn't see his friend standing watch, but James knew Sawyer Hughes well enough to be certain he wouldn't have left their sassy charge alone. As Sawyer's phone kicked over to voice mail, James leaned forward frowning, tossing his phone onto the desk in front of him, he addressed the man sitting in front of the controls, "Run the feed from this camera back ten minutes and time-lapse the replay."

Rapid clicks of the keyboard followed and James watched as the feed replayed in front of him. "Son-of-a-bitch." Tapping the screen, he pointed out, "Watch the bird, it flies from the left to the right." He and his man watched as the same bird made the same flight over and over again, "It's a fucking loop. Someone's tapped our system—switch to the second server." As the man working the monitors typed furiously, James watched in horror as an entirely different picture flashed to the screen.

James's phone rang as he was reaching for it, he was surprised to see Parker's name on the screen but not surprised when his American friend skipped the preliminaries, "I just got a call from Phillip Gaines, Carli's art director. He said Mallory and Robin—his boy-toy—are together and he wanted to warn me because the three of them argued about Carli before they took off from the hotel."

"Someone has tapped our system and looped the security feeds. We just found it, Sawyer is unconscious by the pool and Olivia is missing. The woman you're chasing is obviously a distraction, get everyone back inside—*Now!*" James yelled for his staff to call for back up and to send someone to the pool area. He hit the door at a dead run heading toward the estate's indoor gun range. Sprinting down the damned cobblestone walkway was treacherous and it flashed through his mind the whole thing needed to be replaced in favor of something smoother so it was safer. Shaking off his distracted thoughts, he focused on his efforts to prevent a disaster and hoped upon hope the gut level instinct that sent him this way hadn't been wrong.

Before James cleared the high hedge surrounding Mary Elizabeth's formal gardens the sound of a woman's scream and then two gunshots filled the normally quiet sanctuary. Years of training made it easy for him to distinguish between the sounds and those shots had definitely come from two different guns. Rounding the corner, the first thing he saw was Carli standing in the open doorway, staring blankly at Olivia who lay flat on the small sidewalk—a trail of blood streaming from her shoulder. A man dressed in black was crumbled in a heap to the side of the sidewalk in the grass, James didn't spare him a second glance—the bullet hole just behind his ear told him everything he needed to know.

Mary Elizabeth stepped out of the shadows, a haunted look in her pretty blue eyes, "I couldn't let him take Carli. We heard him say he was going to make sure she was *gone*. She belongs to Tristan and Parker. When Olivia tripped I thought she was safe so I took the shot, but—"

"Give me the gun, sweetheart." Her gun was dangling from her fingers as her arm hung limply at her side, he engaged the safety and tucked it into the back of his pants after she slowly handed it over. It wouldn't matter how warranted her actions had been, James knew the burden of what she'd done would weigh on the loving woman's heart for a very long time. "Help is on the way, Mary Elizabeth, but I need for you to get some towels from inside." When she simply blinked at him, he repeated the words using the tone he'd heard William use when he'd wanted to get his free-spirited wife's attention. James had recognized their Dominant/submissive relationship as soon as he'd met the vivacious couple, it had been one of the reasons he'd felt so comfortable in their company.

Kneeling beside Olivia, James checked her pulse, it was weak but steady, and when she started to stir, he stilled her with a touch, "No, kitten, stay still until I can cover this nasty hole in your shoulder." Mary Elizabeth reappeared at his side seconds later with a huge stack of clean towels and he had to hold back his laughter. Olivia would most certainly bleed to death if they needed the armful of linens she'd handed him. As he pressed the soft towels over her wound, Olivia hissed at the pressure, "I'm sorry, I know it hurts, but we need to stop the bleeding before your brother gets here and has a stroke, kitten."

Rolling her over gently, he wasn't surprised to see a larger hole where the bullet had passed through just under her collarbone. He heard her speak, but the words had been so faint he'd missed them. When he didn't respond, she tried again, "Sawyer...hurt...pool." James's heart clenched, here was a woman who'd just been terrorized by an intruder and shot, but her first concern had been the man who'd been tasked with keeping her safe. James knew Sawyer was going to feel as if he'd failed her, and he hoped Olivia would be able to help his best friend fight his way through the guilt.

Even though she'd lapsed back into unconsciousness, he kissed her forehead and assured her they were already taking care of Sawyer. James looked up just as the entire area swarmed with people. He as relieved to see William Harris catch his lovely wife in mid-air when she launched herself into his arms. Parker looked down at his sister and James swore every ounce of blood in the man's face drained away. Having a man as huge as Parker Daniels standing over them swaying back and forth was a bit unnerving. "She'll be fine, Parker. It's a clean through and through, but we do need to transport her ASAP to check for bone fragments and to minimize infection. I'd say she was hit with a reflex shot." His words had meant to calm Parker, but didn't seem to do the trick—damn, he often forgot the Knights of the Boardroom hadn't been soldiers, despite their preference for hiring them. "Call for the medivac, Parker, then see to your woman."

Parker seemed to snap out of his stupor and turned his attention to James. He heard the desperate hope in Parker's voice when he asked, "You're sure she'll be alright? Jesus, I don't know what I'd do if anything happened to her." James nodded and Parker pushed on, "The chopper is already on its way, Sawyer has a nasty concussion, it looks like somebody tried to bust open the back of his head with the butt of a gun. Christ he's going to be pissed when they shave his head to stitch him up—vain bastard." They all teased Sawyer about his hair, his surfer boy blond streaks and longer cut always made him look younger than James knew he was. But it was the citron green eyes framed by lashes James knew women drooled over were what made women follow Sawyer Hughes around like puppies.

Olivia Daniels was the first woman James had ever known who'd stood up to Sawyer and he'd laughed out loud the first time she'd put her hands on her hips, and tapped her foot impatiently as she listened to Sawyer drone on about her safety. She'd finally held up her hand signaling him to stop and proceeded to explain in colorful detail all the reasons she thought he was an overbearing buffoon. The look on Sawyer's face had been priceless as he looked back at her in confusion. Sawyer had looked at James and asked, "Is she for real? And what the fuck is a buffoon anyway?"

Yeah, Sawyer would probably pitch a fit about them cutting his hair, but all things considered, his best friend was lucky he wasn't laying in the grass like the asswipe who'd hit him. Parker knelt beside his sister brushing his fingers gently over the abrasions on her cheek, "I wish I could kill him again, shortcake, but it looks like Tristan's mom did a mighty fine job all by herself."

Olivia's eyes fluttered open and filled with tears as she looked up at her brother, "He was going to kill Carli. I tried to stall so you could get to us, but it didn't work. I'm sorry. My arm feels weird. I'm tired." Tears ran into her hair as her lashes fluttered back closed laying softly against her cheeks.

"Parker, I've got her, go check on Carli—from what I saw she was badly shaken." James knew Tristan had carried her to the side, sitting with her on his lap so she wasn't facing the dead man still laying lifeless in plain view. James hoped the police would cover him up when they arrived, because the sight was starting to bother even the most hardened of them. He was relieved to hear the telltale *thump-thump* of the incoming medevac helicopter.

James stopped the paramedics as they started to load Olivia, he leaned down whispering against the shell of her ear, "You'll not escape us this easily, kitten—we have plans for you. Very hot, very kinky plans."

The whole world seemed to brighten when he saw the seductive smile lift the corners of her lips as she sighed, "Thank God."

THE HORRIFIC SCENE kept playing over in Carli's mind until she was sure she was losing her mind. Every time she closed her eyes she heard the guns discharge, watched Olivia fall to the ground and the man's arm came up, his gun discharging when his head jerked to the side a bright red mist flying from the other side. She shuddered in Tristan's arms as they sat in a private waiting room at the large hospital. They'd stayed downstairs until the media circus forced the hospital staff to move them into a more secluded area.

Carli wondered how newspaper editors were going to fit everything into their headlines...*Member of Queen's Extended Family Kills Scottish National While Defending American Supermodel and Oil Heiress Turned Spy on the Run.* Yep, that ought to about cover it. She'd been in shock for a while after the incident at the estate, but she was finally starting to feel more connected to everything going on around her. She'd spoken with her sister on the phone for several minutes and remembering what Robin MacDonald had done to Cressida helped her put his death into perspective.

By the time they made their way to Tristan's parents' London penthouse she'd been so tired she'd barely made it to the bed after her shower before her body had simply collapsed. But even physical exhaustion hadn't kept the sights and sounds of the previous afternoon from replaying in her mind. She didn't think any of them got much sleep, and they'd returned to the hospital early the next morning. Sitting in the small waiting room, Carli was relieved to see Phillip walk through the door. She was glad he'd made his way through the media circus still camped outside the hospital, and she'd held his hand as he'd told Tristan and Parker everything he'd discovered when he'd looked through Robin's email account.

Phillip apologized to her repeatedly, blaming himself for Robin and Mallory's scheming. He'd used Carli as an excuse for not committing to Robin, "He wasn't husband material, he was just a dalliance—but I shouldn't have used you as my excuse. I had no idea he thought he could just substitute Mallory for you, and good Lord, it makes me shudder to think about having sex with that heathen woman." It was the first time Carli had laughed since the shooting and it felt good to let go of some of the tension all the trauma had brought into her life.

"Well, that heathen woman is going to find out my father isn't a man to be trifled with, he's made enough calls she'll have a hell of a time finding anyone to represent her in court. Personally I'd like to see her rot in jail." Carli knew Tristan had also been making calls and she wondered if Mallory had any clue she'd made such powerful enemies.

Carli hadn't planned to continue on with the upcoming photo shoots, but when Olivia got wind of her plan she'd been livid and quickly convinced Carli otherwise, "Oh no you don't, you aren't letting that worthless piece of ninja shit keep you from doing what you love. I heard the guys talking about you going to Brazil to do a spread for the upcoming World Cup and Summer Olympics—you think I want people thinking I'm the reason you snubbed the world's most popular sport? Nope, not happening, so you get your happy ass on that plane and let my brother and his kinky sidekick over there fly you to Rio. Damn, I wish I could go with you."

Carli had smiled when she saw James leaning against the doorframe, "Kitten, we're going to have a serious conversation about your language."

Parker stepped around him to enter the room and

laughed, "Good luck with that, my friend, I've been nagging her about the same thing since she was in junior high. Ask her sometime why she was nearly expelled from her magnet school."

"Semantics, dear brother. It wasn't my fault the professor disagreed with my creative use of the English language—he had no imagination. And I've already thanked Brodie for helping me out—so can the review of my academic career, big brother." Their sibling banter was exactly what she needed—the familiarity of it settled her and she knew their sparring had been partially for her benefit and she appreciated the fact they'd made the effort to distract her.

Tristan stepped up behind her and enfolded her in his arms, *"Mon cher,* the car is waiting downstairs. Phillip has your shoot set up, we'll stop there on our way to the airport. He assures us you're a wonder and will breeze right through it." Carli wanted to laugh, everyone thought it was all about her, but her wardrobe, hair and makeup teams were really the ones who made her look amazing. She just smiled and held still while Phillip and the photographer worked their magic.

After saying their goodbyes, Carli walked between Parker and Tristan as they made their way down the long hospital corridor toward the back elevator. Just before the doors slid closed, she heard Sawyer Hughes shout, "You fucking shaved the back of my head? For a few lousy stitches?" Both Parker and Tristan burst out laughing, and for the first time in longer than she could remember, Carli felt like everything was right in her world.

Epilogue

Three Weeks Later...

OLIVIA DANIELS PACED the length of James Mikels' living room muttering to herself, "I'm tired of being cooped up in this damned house. I can't do anything wearing this stupid sling, and who the hell turned off the Wi-Fi? That was just fucking mean." James and Sawyer had both been livid when they found out she'd been working because they'd worried she would compromise her safety by revealing her location—obviously they didn't think she was bright enough to keep herself out of trouble. *Well, Ms. Genius, you did manage to get yourself in a pretty big mess in a remarkably short period of time.*

It had taken her less than six months after agreeing to help the CIA track the progress of nuclear programs in several unstable nations for her life to spiral so far out of control it was barely recognizable. But she'd been so busy tracking down the information her superiors wanted, she hadn't been watching her own backdoor, and whoever had hacked her files hadn't spent much time trying to hide their meddling.

Gathering information for the CIA had turned out to be surprisingly easy. Much to her surprise, the prejudices she'd been fighting for as long as she could remember had suddenly been huge assets. Sitting in coffee shops and bars with fellow students and coworkers, Olivia had listened to people make blonde jokes, ridicule geeks as only knowing *their* subject, and roll their eyes at *short people* because they were assumed to be inferior in some way no one ever seemed to want to identify. Hell, she was all of those things and those characteristics had finally played in her favor for a change. No one had seen her as a threat—they'd made every conceivable excuse to hit on her, but they hadn't seen her as a security problem...or so she'd thought.

Stopping to stare longingly out the window out over the large estate in the direction of the swimming pool, Olivia wished she could lose herself in the rigors of her favorite exercise, there was nothing better than complete physical exhaustion as a sleeping aid—except maybe a few soul shattering orgasms...but hell, she wasn't getting any of those either. In fact, if the information she'd been reading in the books she'd pilfered from James's library was right, she probably hadn't ever experienced that sort of release.

She'd been so sure she hadn't dreamt James's whispered words before they'd loaded her aboard the medevac helicopter, but she certainly hadn't seen any evidence of his promise they had kinky plans for her wasn't just the hopeful creation of her mind. *Damn it, I really need to stop wishing for something that isn't going to happen. Just move on already, Liv.* Her brother, Carli, and Tristan were due to arrive at her parents' home outside Houston any day, so she'd be safe there. Without access to her computer and the internet, she certainly wasn't making any progress finding out who had manipulated her files and until she found out *who*, she certainly couldn't find out *why*.

Decision made, Olivia sent a quick email to her father asking for his help getting home. She'd copied the request to his assistant, knowing she'd be the one to make the arrangements. Hopefully her brother hadn't already warned them against helping her. Within seconds she noticed a reply, but groaned when she saw it was from Parker—damn it to dusty doorknobs, she should have known he'd hack her email account. *Not happening, little sister—stay put. Do James and Sawyer know you're trying to give them the slip?* Olivia would peg the chances of him not ratting her out to...well, everybody—at somewhere between infinitesimal and nonexistent. Fuck me, this is not going to end well for me on any level.

Olivia's cell phone pinged with an incoming message just as the front door opened, she heard James and Sawyer exchanging greetings with the butler as she slid her finger over the screen to read the message. *You didn't think you could hide, did you? Treason is a very serious offense, Olivia.* Several pictures followed—pictures of everyone she loved...her parents, her grandmother, and her brother. Each picture was date stamped and had been taken within the past week. *If we can find them, we can find you.* Everything around her started to spin and suddenly it felt as if all the air had been sucked from the room. Over the roar in her ears she barely heard someone shouting her name, but she was falling down a long dark tunnel and knew they'd never hear if she answered...so she didn't bother, she just let the darkness wash over her.

The End

Books by Avery Gale

The Wolf Pack Series
Mated
Fated Magic
Tempted by Darkness

Masters of the Prairie Winds Club
Out of the Storm
Saving Grace
Jen's Journey
Bound Treasure
Punishing for Pleasure
Accidental Trifecta
Missionary Position

Standalones
Taking Out the Mother of the Bride and other Christmas Wishes

Knights of the Boardroom
Knights of the Boardroom Book One
Knights of the Boardroom Book Two
Knights of the Boardroom Book Three
(With Bonus Novella, *Lighting Up Valentine's Day*)

I would love to hear from you!

Email:

avery.gale@ymail.com

Website:

www.averygalebooks.com/index.html

Facebook:

facebook.com/avery.gale.3

Instagram:

avery.gale

Twitter:

@avery_gale

Excerpt from Tempted by Darkness

The Wolf Pack, Book Three

Avery Gale

KIT AND BRADEN rode in silence to the open field where Aradia was said to have been buried. There was no marker per the Queen of Witches request, she'd known her gravesite would become a contentious memorial and she'd been adamantly opposed to the idea. Fearing future persecution of those who would follow, the wise witch had demanded the exact location of her grave never be revealed. From everything Kit had read about the woman, considered the Queen of Witches, she'd been a firm believer in living for the future rather than in the past. Every witch's Book of Shadows contained bits of wisdom attributed to Aradia that had been passed down generation to generation for countless centuries. Kit's favorite was the reminder never to be humbled so much that you stumbled over our own past.

As they exited the small rental car, Braden looked over at her and winked, "Remember, individually we are good, but together we are superheroes. And Granny Good Witch promised me a cape when we get Angie back." When she cast him a sidelong glance, he chuckled, "What? I know I can't fly with a cape, but it will be fun to mess with the kids back at the estate." She shook her head, in so many ways he was an adult, but there were still moments when the childhood he'd missed bubbled to the surface. Everyone at the estate relished those moments because in their minds it meant he was healing and maturing into the powerful wizard he was destined to become.

Braden's childhood had been cut far too short because he'd been the focus of Damian's obsession from the time the dark wizard learned the child was his grandson. Braden's father had run away with him after the young boy's mother was killed. For years, father and son had barely managed to stay one-step ahead of the man obsessed with the young boy, but their luck had finally run out and Braden lost his father too.

As the sun started to sink beneath the horizon, a brilliant ball of orange light shimmered several feet in front of where Kit and Braden stood waiting. For several seconds the light simply hovered and spun slowly around and Kit wondered if it was ensuring they'd come alone. When Devin finally emerged as an ill-defined mist, he scanned the area before focusing on the two of them. Just as Kit opened her mouth to demand he give them proof Angie was still alive, she appeared next to him.

"What the hell is that?" Braden started to step forward as he spoke but Kit placed her hand on his shoulder to hold him back. Devin's posture had shifted immediately and Kit was worried about the young man's safety. Even though Angie appeared to be trapped in some sort of glass bubble, she appeared to be unharmed. Braden turned back to Devin and took a menacing step forward before Kit pulled him back once again. "Can she hear us?" Just then they saw Angie waving her arms and she looked as though she was shouting but they couldn't hear anything. "Well, guess that answers that question. Hey, how long can she stay in there without fresh air?" Kit wanted to roll her eyes, leave it to

Braden to shift so quickly to logical and scientific observations. Good Goddess it was certainly easy to see he and Angie were related. Kit was far more worried that none of them were going to live long enough for oxygen to ever be an issue.

"Don't worry about the bubble. It is soundproof, but she will not come to any harm being in there. She had been treated well as I'm sure she will tell you, assuming you are willing to negotiate with me." Kit's interest was piqued because Devin had emphasized the word *me* and she found it odd he'd make that distinction.

'What do you make of this, Kit? Why did he say we are negotiating with him? Do you think we were right the last time when we sensed his reluctance to be his brother's lackey?'

Kit appreciated the telepathic link she and Braden had established. They'd spent many hours practicing the silent method of communication and she was grateful they shared a way to speak without being heard. *'I was just thinking the same thing. Let's see where this takes us, shall we?'*

Returning her focus to Devin, Kit demanded, "Tell us what you want. Why would you want to kidnap Angie? And who was responsible?" Devin rolled his eyes at her questions and it quickly became clear to Kit that Devin wasn't particularly interested in discussing the details.

"I can't tell you everything—at least not yet, but you already know that. And I'm sure you have already figured out that my brother wants to trade the good doctor for his grandson." When she opened her mouth to speak, he held up his hand in a silent gesture silencing her. "I already know that isn't going to happen and in truth I'd be somewhat disappointed in you if you agreed to such an exchange. Remember, I said your negotiations are with me, not my brother." For the first time in days, Kit felt some of the tension leave her body as the possibility that they might get Angie back without extreme violence loomed before her.

During the next half hour, Devin paced so quickly along a line in front of them that he literally wore a path in the grass beneath his feet. There were times as he spoke that Kit wondered if he was still speaking to them or he'd simply become lost in his own thoughts. Devin outlined his brother's plan to take over the Supreme Council after he was freed from behind the sealed portal—and realizing how close Damian was to making it happen scared Kit more than she wanted to admit.

"Kit, the magic you used the night you sent Damian behind the seal was dark, very dark. And the remarkable thing is you were completely untrained. I know the powers that be are telling you they don't know how you managed it, but that isn't exactly true. They know it was dark magic, what they don't know is how you learned it. Whether it's innate knowledge or simply natural ability, then they have a really big problem on their hands."

"Explain why they consider it their problem." As much as Kit wanted to deny his words, she honestly wasn't sure she could. Something about his observation resonated in her soul as the truth. She didn't like it, but she'd never been one to deny reality even if it didn't fit well with the way she wanted to see herself. Her passionate response to Jameson's dominance that first night at the club was a perfect example. As much as she had wanted to be outraged by his high-handed behavior, she hadn't been able to deny her body's intense response to his dominance.

"There is a battle coming, Kit, you already know this, but what may surprise you is how quickly the scales are tipping in Damian's favor."

Excerpt from Missionary Position

Masters of the Prairie Winds Club, Book Seven
Avery Gale

BY THE TIME Peter and Fischer escorted her to where their friends were already celebrating, Lara was about ready to faint. She hated being in trouble—she always had. But hearing Tobi's and Gracie's giggling had provided the perfect distraction, she felt herself relax as she took what felt like her first deep breath since she'd stepped between her two Masters several minutes earlier. The men had stepped to the side shaking their heads as if women were the most confusing creatures on the planet, and Lara was more than happy to join her friends. By the time Tobi and Gracie had finished recounting Lilly's outrageous behavior, Lara had been laughing so hard she'd had to retrieve a napkin from the bar to dry her eyes.

She'd never lived in one place long enough to form any real friendships while growing up, so she'd been completely unprepared for all the shifting social dynamics of the world of teenage girls when she'd started pubic school as a freshman. It wasn't until she'd met the two women standing beside her that Lara had really started to understand the joy of being surrounded by good friends.

Tobi and Gracie winced when Lara told them what

had taken place on the other side of the room. "Oh, girlfriend, you are in for it." Unconsciously rubbing her ass, Tobi shook her head, "I know from experience that cell phones are a cardinal sin...and just FYI, the same is true of iPads, anything with a camera is gonna get your ass in a pickle...or strapped to a spanking bench. Hell hath no fury like a Dom with a legitimate complaint."

"Yeah, not the brightest crayon in the box this one," Gracie added, using her thumb to indicate Tobi," she thought she could cut through the club with her iPad on, but even though she was working on an order for the Forum shops, Master Micah's cameras don't miss anything."

"Yep, the rat-fink sent the video clip to both Kyle and Kent. Damn those Doms stick together like glue. Anyway, I'd already lost my cell phone for a month, and damned if they didn't take my iPad for two months." The gleam in Tobi's eyes told Lara there was more to the story, so she just waited. "But I got even with them. I went shopping with Lilly." Evidently Lara's puzzled expression was enough to prompt another round of giggles.

Gracie leaned close and whispered, "When Lilly found out what her sons had done, she intentionally *misplaced* her phone about five minutes into their shopping trip. They were gone all day and no one could contact them."

"Of course, we'd forgotten about our bracelets." Lara knew the three women had specially designed jewelry with small tracking devices as an added layer of security. Tobi sighed and shook her head. "Boy I'm telling you, when the four of them stalked through Jezebel, everybody, and I do mean every single person in that restaurant, stopped what they were doing and watched the show." Tobi shuddered and Lara found herself dying to hear the rest of the story, but something about the way Kyle West had just looked at her from across the room set off all her internal alarms. Tobi and Gracie both followed her gaze, and Lara heard Tobi's whispered, "Oh no, I wonder what's happened. I know that look…and it never heralds good news."

Lara watched as the men conversed among themselves. Several pulled out their phones and spoke animatedly, their gazes flickering in her direction. But it was Peter's and Fischer's expressions that worried her the most, their eyes held something between worry and sympathy, and it was the most terrifying thing she'd ever seen. Lara felt Tobi and Gracie flank her, their arms going around her protectively as she started trembling so hard she wondered if she would shake apart.

The sound of her own heartbeat pounded so loudly in her ears it nearly drowned out the harsh sound of her gasping for breath. Lara saw both Peter and Fischer turn at the same moment to look at her as if they'd heard her mind racing as worry assailed her. For the first time, Lara understood the fear her grandparents must have lived with every time a stranger appeared on their front porch. Their daughter and her family had been traipsing all over the world and she knew they had to have worried themselves sick. Good God, she really was losing it if she was thinking about people she hadn't seen in almost a decade. Frantically reaching for her phone, Lara realized it was no longer in her pocket. Why hadn't she answered it or at least checked it? Anyone who would have called her was already in the room—everyone but those few people who'd been given her number as an emergency number for her parents. The horrible realization that washed over her made her knees buckle, and the last thing she remembered was the sound of chaos surrounding her.

Made in the USA
Middletown, DE
13 May 2019